Unclaimed
Heart

Unclaimed Heart

Kim Wilkins

razOr
bill

Unclaimed Heart

RAZORBILL

Published by the Penguin Group
Penguin Young Readers Group
345 Hudson Street, New York, New York 10014, U.S.A.
Penguin Group (USA) Inc., 375 Hudson Street, New York, New York 10014, U.S.A.
Penguin Group (Canada), 90 Eglinton Avenue East, Suite 700,
Toronto, Ontario, Canada M4P 2Y3 (a division of Pearson Penguin Canada Inc.)
Penguin Books Ltd, 80 Strand, London WC2R 0RL, England
Penguin Ireland, 25 St Stephen's Green, Dublin 2, Ireland (a division of Penguin Books Ltd)
Penguin Group (Australia), 250 Camberwell Road, Camberwell,
Victoria 3124, Australia (a division of Pearson Australia Group Pty Ltd)
Penguin Books India Pvt Ltd, 11 Community Centre,
Panchsheel Park, New Delhi – 110 017, India
Penguin Group (NZ), 67 Apollo Drive, Rosedale, North Shore 0632, New Zealand
(a division of Pearson New Zealand Ltd.)

Penguin Books (South Africa) (Pty) Ltd, 24 Sturdee Avenue,
Rosebank, Johannesburg 2196, South Africa

Penguin Books Ltd, Registered Offices: 80 Strand, London WC2R 0RL, England

First published as *The Pearl Hunters* by Omnibus Books, Ltd 2008

10 9 8 7 6 5 4 3 2 1

LIBRARY OF CONGRESS CATALOGING-IN-PUBLICATION DATA IS AVAILABLE

Wilkins, Kim
Unclaimed Heart/by Kim Wilkins
p. cm.
Summary: In 1799, having stowed away on her father's ship sailing
from Dartmouth,England to Ceylon in search of her long-lost mother,
seventeen-year-old Constance Blackchurch falls in love with a nineteen-year-old
French orphan they rescue from a nefarious pearl dealer.

ISBN 978-1-59514-258-0
[1. Love—Fiction 2. Social Classes—Fiction 3. Fathers and Daughters—Fiction
4. Missing Persons—Fiction 5. British—Sri Lanka—Fiction 6. Orphans—Fiction
8. Sri Lanka—History—18th Century—Fiction 9. Sea Stories]
PZ7.W64867 Unc 2009
[Fic]22

Printed in the United States of America

For Astrid

Chapter 1

DARTMOUTH, ENGLAND: 1799

Constance burst into the sunlight and began the last dash towards home from Dr. Poole's: precisely where she wasn't supposed to be. She was supposed to be at French lessons, not studying astronomy. She could see the pale grey exterior of Aunty Violet's house, the lavender bushes sunning themselves. *Aunty Violet.* Constance felt a pang of shame, thinking about her own behavior earlier that morning.

"Mademoiselle Girard is horrid to me!" Constance had protested. "I don't care to learn French; we are at war with them. I speak it passably well already, so I don't see why I should endure her."

"Constance, so many young women would be envious of your education."

"I'm grateful for my education, but won't sit for another minute with that cross old harpy while she shouts at me for putting my adjectives in the wrong place."

"There's no arguing about this, Constance."

So she hadn't argued; she'd just run off. Which would not have put her in a panic under ordinary circumstances. Ordinarily she would have returned sheepishly at dinner time, apologized, and then resumed French lessons. Today, however, circumstances had become far from ordinary.

Dr. Poole had lifted his head from the map of constellations and offered to fetch tea. He'd only been gone a minute when he returned with a smile twitching at his lips. "Constance, I believe I've seen your father's ship."

A jolt of white heat had leapt into her heart. *Father!* She raced to Dr. Poole's front room, which had a view down to the estuary. There at the quayside was, indeed, *Good Bess*, a ninety-foot merchantman with a gold-leaf taffrail and elegant oriel windows, the red duster of the British merchant fleet flying proudly from the masthead. From this distance, Constance could see a few dark figures moving around on it. When had it arrived? Was Father already home, hearing from Aunty Violet how rude and willful she'd been that morning? Good grief, what if Mademoiselle Girard was there, pouring poison into his ear about what a bad student she was?

That's when she had started running.

Constance paused at the front path, panting. She strained her ears. Yes, that was Father's booming voice all right, though she couldn't make out what he was saying. Her stomach turned to water. He came to see her so rarely that he took on mythical size and power in her imagination. She hurried inside, caught her reflection in the glass at the entrance hall and realized immediately that she couldn't greet her father in this state: eyes wild, cheeks flushed, hair loose. Perspiration had soaked through her chemise and made the muslin of her dress almost see-through. She did not resemble even remotely the respectable merchant's daughter that her father expected to see. The only thing for it was to go upstairs, change and brush her hair.

But before she could turn towards the stairs, footsteps approached. She ducked into the morning room. Then, when the footsteps drew closer, she slid behind the heavily embroidered curtains, heart thudding, books still pressed against her chest.

Father entered the room, followed by Aunty Violet.

"What does it say?" Aunty Violet asked. "Henry, you've gone quite pale. What does it say?"

There was a rustle of paper, and Constance remembered the letter that had arrived for Father a week before, all the way from Ceylon. She had assumed it to be about tea, one of Father's chief trading stocks. But perhaps it contained other, more interesting, information. She listened, puzzled.

"It's from an old friend," Father said gruffly. "William Howlett. I . . . he knew me before. . . ." He trailed off. Constance couldn't remember him ever sounding so uncertain, so vulnerable.

"Sit, Henry," Aunty Violet said. "I'll get you a dram of rum. Then, when you've calmed yourself, perhaps you can tell me what that letter contained that upset you so."

Minutes passed. Constance held very still. The heavy curtain prevented the heat leaving her skin, and the stuffy air clogged her lungs. Aunty Violet returned, and a moment later Father spoke.

"Howlett has lately taken up residence in a small port town called Nagakodi, in the north of Ceylon. He has heard news of Faith."

Constance's breath stopped in her throat.

"The locals have stories about a woman named Blackchurch, who came into the port some years ago."

Faith Blackchurch. Her mother. She had been gone for

sixteen years. Constance had not noticed her mysterious disappearance initially, as she was only a baby at the time. But as she grew older, she had become fixated by the details, reluctantly related by Aunty Violet. Faith had complained of a headache, and went to sleep in the guest room on the garden side of the house. Sometime in the night there had been a wild storm, and when Father had awoken in the morning she was gone. The front door had been left open, and two sets of footprints had led away through the mud to the road. Despite the police's best efforts, despite the expensive private investigation Henry had ordered, nobody had heard from her again.

Until now.

Constance's mind was electrified by the idea. For years she had dared to believe that her mother was still alive somewhere. And now it seemed she might be proved right. Her already hot blood warmed further. Behind the heavy curtain, she grew extremely uncomfortable.

"Some years ago?" Aunty Violet asked dubiously. "How many years? Who's to say where she went after that?"

"It doesn't matter," Father replied hotly. "It's the first we've ever heard of her. We know she didn't die that night, that she lived long enough to get to Ceylon at least."

"Henry—"

"As soon as *Good Bess* is unloaded, I'll be taking her back out."

"All the way to Ceylon? You're chasing a dream, Henry."

Constance realized she was starting to feel dizzy. She tried to shift her weight, to lean herself against the window sill. As she did so, one of the books she was holding slid from her grasp, landing with a thump on the floor. Her heart stopped. Footsteps. The curtain was flung back, and she found herself gaze to gaze with her father.

It had long troubled her that she had inherited Father's coloring: brown eyes, olive skin, auburn hair. The only thing she had of her mother's was height: she was precisely at her father's eye level.

"Good day, Constance," he said sternly. He bent to pick up her book, glancing at the cover before handing it back to her. "Astronomy, still?"

This was his way—to treat her interests as though they were as trivial as a small child's. She railed. "The order and motion of the heavenly bodies is rather a large topic, Father. It may take some time for me to tire of it."

"As I understand it, the language and grammar of France is also rather a large topic. And yet you've abandoned that prematurely. It's certainly a more suitable field of study for a young woman."

Constance felt shame flush her cheeks, and glanced quickly at Aunty Violet, who offered an apologetic smile.

Constance and her father paused in that position a moment, head to head, the book offered across the tight, tense space. Then Constance took her book and nodded. "Welcome home, Father."

"I will see you at supper, child. Forget what you heard, for indeed you were not intended to hear it." He turned on his heel and left, with Aunty Violet scurrying after him.

Constance took a deep breath and sat heavily in the window sill, her mind ablaze with the possibilities. Did he really think it possible for her to forget what she had heard?

"She's seventeen, Henry. I think you should just tell her the truth."

Henry Blackchurch leaned both fists, knuckles down, on the back of Violet's sofa and shook his head vehemently. "We don't know what the truth is."

Violet's voice softened. "We know enough, surely."

His eyes went to the window. Outside, the summer light had finally faded. The night was soft and starry. "We can only speculate."

"She thinks her mother was a saint. As a child she spoke of nothing else but Mother coming home to be with her. I don't know if she still thinks such things. She keeps her feelings to herself. But it's a vulnerable age; she hovers between childhood and womanhood. Her feelings are not in her control."

Henry straightened and nodded towards Alice the maid, who was setting a silver tea tray on the low table. "Leave us, please," he said.

Alice nodded dutifully and slipped out of the sitting room, closing the door behind her. Henry found it difficult to speak of personal matters, even to his sister. Another presence in the room would tie his tongue completely. He folded his hands behind his back and rocked on the balls of his feet. Violet waited patiently.

"I know my wife was . . ." He stopped, started again. "She had flaws."

Violet snorted a derisive laugh.

"But she was my wife, and it's my duty to determine what happened to her, and bring her home if that is her wish. I need you to keep Constance distracted. Don't let her think too much about where I am, or what I am doing. For, truly, she may be disappointed."

"She *will* be disappointed. You both will."

"I can't bring myself to judge Faith as harshly as you, Violet," Henry said. "What if you are wrong?"

Violet shrugged, conceding. "You do what you must, Henry, and we will be here at the end of it, as we always are."

Henry opened the window and leaned out. The sea called, as it had always called him, since he was a young lad. He felt trapped on land, helpless. Out there, he could move. Towards Faith, perhaps. Towards the truth.

"I'll leave on the first favorable tide," he said. "I can't stand still a moment longer."

"Are you coming to bed, Constance?"

Constance turned to the soft hand on her shoulder and smiled weakly at her cousin Daphne. "Momentarily."

Daphne sat on the top step next to Constance, folding her hands in her lap. She had in her hands one of the little novels she liked to read: ghastly romances about beautiful orphans, inevitably trapped in ruined castles while ghosts rattled chains nearby. Constance was always mocking her for her tastes—goodnaturedly, of course.

It was dim in the stairwell, with only the lantern at Constance's feet to illuminate the space. Mother's portrait was directly in front of them, at the bend in the staircase. Constance had often studied this portrait, wondered about her mother, wanted to know her mind, her heart. As a child, she had made up many games about her mother's return, earnestly scribbled stories about her adventures on the road home to her daughter.

Softly, the voices of her father and aunt drifted up the stairs, but she couldn't hear what they were saying.

"What's on your mind, cousin?" Daphne asked.

"Father has news of my mother."

Daphne's eyes widened, her pupils growing large. "Truly?"

"She was seen in Ceylon, some years past." Constance smiled weakly. "That is all I know, as Father will not speak another word of it to me."

"How perfectly thrilling," Daphne breathed, then turned her eyes to Faith Blackchurch's portrait. "She was very beautiful."

"Yes, she was." Constance smiled. Her mother's hair was black as a raven's wing around her oval face, her eyes dark blue and her skin porcelain. In the portrait, she wore a dress of deep crimson and a gold locket around her neck. "You know, I've often wondered if she carried a little portrait in that locket." She didn't want to sound sentimental, so she didn't confess to Daphne that she'd long imagined a picture of herself as a baby shut inside that gold oval.

"Do you remember her at all?"

Constance shook her head. "No, not at all. I try to think back as far as I can. But I only remember Aunty Violet. You." She squeezed her cousin's hand. "I hardly remember Father; he was never around. When he was, all he wanted to do with me was tie knots and learn sailing terms. You know he's leaving again, immediately. Off to Ceylon."

Daphne shuddered with excitement. "To find his lost wife. It's like a book, isn't it?"

"Not the kind of books I read," Constance teased.

"If this were a book, you'd go too, Constance," Daphne said. "You'd stow away and have adventures at sea, meet some noble man posing as a peasant, be reunited with your mother . . . and your father would be revealed as a tyrant, perhaps not even your real father." She checked herself. Her cheeks were growing flushed with excitement. "I'm sorry, cousin. My imagination ran away with me."

Constance patted her knee. "You read too many of those horrid novels."

"I like them horrid."

Constance rose and offered a hand to help Daphne to her feet. "I don't know how you don't have nightmares. This isn't a novel, Daphne. This is my dull, dull life."

And yet she couldn't sleep. Daphne had unwittingly sown a seed that had worked its way into her brain and germinated. Father wasn't taking passengers out on this hastily arranged voyage. Plenty of room for her. Before he realized she was on board, they could be miles from British waters. Too far to turn back.

In the dark, while Daphne breathed deeply and softly in the bed next to her, a plan began to form.

Chapter 2

GULF OF MANNAR, SOUTHERN INDIA: 1799

The movement of sunlight in the water had always fascinated Alexandre Sans-Nom. He sank down and down on his rope, with a stone tied to his back. He had worked pearl banks all along the coasts of India and Ceylon, and knew precisely what to do. With his little pick, he quickly began to loosen oysters from their sticking places and drop them in his bag. Two other divers worked with him: Sinhalese men whom Gilbert de Locke had employed two weeks ago in Marichchakuddu. Alexandre knew that de Locke didn't like to keep divers on for too many months. They became lazy, he said. They were more likely to turn to stealing. He kept only Alexandre: for eight years now.

The Sinhalese divers pulled their ropes and returned to the surface. One minute was the average amount of time that a diver could stay at nine fathoms, airless, under the weight of the green ocean. Alexandre could stay far longer, four or five minutes. Until his lungs felt hard, and dizzy spangles began to gather on the edges of his vision. Then he'd pull the rope and be hauled to the surface, gasping, with four times as many oysters as his companions.

"Well done, lad," de Locke said to him, with a tight smile that might have been pride. Was it a misplaced paternal feeling that kept Alexandre in de Locke's employ? Or was it simply Alexandre's uncanny ability to hold his breath for so long? After all, that was the circumstance around which they had found each other.

He was sleeping on a mattress, under the caravan where he worked when he first heard them.

"The boy is not for sale," said Givot, the caravan's owner.

"I will pay you what he's worth to you. Autumn is only three weeks away, and then winter will follow. Your show will be off the road; you'll be paying his keep for no return."

Givot harrumphed, and Alexandre felt a warm discomfort creeping over his skin. Were they talking about him? He felt vulnerable, as though he might be in trouble. Last time he had been in trouble, Givot had whipped him twice across the back with his horsewhip.

"Where did you find him?" the mysterious voice asked.

Givot, who loved the sound of his own voice, launched into a tale that the eleven-year-old Alexandre had never heard before. "His mother sold him to me when he was two. She was poor, couldn't keep him. Tried to drown him in a laundry tub. When he stopped fighting, she pulled him up. He took a breath and kept right on breathing."

A chill spread through his stomach. Was this true? Givot had always told him that his parents were scholars, studying at the university in Paris. That, one day, when they had finished their studies, they would return for him. Until then, they had given strict instructions that Givot was to care for him, and he was to do whatever was bid him.

The stranger was still talking. "This is my final offer. I know you could use the money. Your horses are looking tired and old."

"I won't hear of it."

Alexandre blocked his ears with his hands so he wouldn't hear the rest of the argument, the two men talking about him as though he were only as important as a horse. He curled on his side and held in sobs, a pit of emptiness opening up within him. He belonged nowhere, with no one. Sleep eluded him.

Hours later, after all the lanterns had been extinguished, quiet footsteps had alerted him to somebody's presence nearby.

Gilbert de Locke crouched next to the caravan, leaning his head to seek Alexandre out. "Boy?" he whispered. "You should come with me."

Alexandre, small and frightened, had become paralyzed.

"I will take you somewhere warm and sunny. I will pay you handsomely."

Only the first part of de Locke's promise came true. The coast of India was indeed warm and sunny, but it seemed that de Locke forgot his offer of payment almost as soon as Alexandre had taken his hand and agreed to follow him. Being young, never having known anything but hardship, he didn't complain.

———

Down he went again, the two Sinhalese divers beside him. He worked as quickly as he could, waiting for his companions to be pulled up. Then he spun in a slow circle to make sure he was alone, his dark hair floating around his face. Baroque undersea formations surrounded him;

only fishes watched. He reached for an oyster, wishing his fingertips could see inside. Aware that he had only limited time, he pried it open with his pick. Nothing. Another, and another. Nothing. The cracked shells spun slowly away from him, towards the ocean floor. Shadows of the other divers appeared above; he returned to his original task, collecting oysters for de Locke. One day he would find a pearl, in those brief moments alone under the sea. And when he did, he would run away from Gilbert de Locke and buy a passage home to France. He would show de Locke that he was no longer the naive boy he had once been.

———

Gilbert de Locke poured three generous glasses of claret. One for himself, and one each for Arthur Petty and his wife, who sat on the sofa with a box of pearls between them. Arthur took the drink happily, but Mrs. Petty left hers sitting on the side table as she prodded the pearls, a disdainful expression pinching her nose. She needed a pair of pearls for earrings, but nothing was good enough for her.

How de Locke hated the English.

Arthur left his wife choosing pearls and joined de Locke at the window, his shoes clicking on the parquetry floor.

"Do you deal with English traders at all, Mr. de Locke? I'm sorry, *Monsieur* de Locke."

"All nationalities," de Locke replied, "though England dominates the merchant marine."

"We came out of Dartmouth two years ago on an English merchant vessel," Arthur said. "Henry Blackchurch. Do you know him?"

De Locke took a gulp of claret. "No, I don't," he lied. He didn't tell Arthur Petty that Henry Blackchurch, with his bluster and his temper and his self-importance, was the reason he had started hating the English in the first place. Instead, he kept his eyes on the storm.

"A fine fellow," Arthur continued. "A true gentleman."

"How do you do there, Mrs. Petty?" de Locke asked, changing the subject.

"I've found a pair that go tolerably well. I dare say they might make a fine pair of earrings, though I can see on close inspection that they are not identical."

"Never mind, dear," Arthur said, "your head between them will provide a distraction."

De Locke swallowed a bark of laughter. Thunder boomed and rolled over the villa.

"Quickly now, dear," Arthur said. "There's a storm

on the way." He turned to de Locke. "Don't you worry about your vessel out there in the bad weather?"

"Oh, no, *La Reine des Perles* is a solid schooner." His eyes returned to the window again. "Besides, one of my crew sleeps on board. He"ll take care of her."

"A native fellow? Can they be trusted?" Arthur said, his mouth turning down haughtily.

"Oh, the natives are trustworthy," de Locke said, resisting the urge to say they were easily more trustworthy than the English. "But my lad is French. Alexandre Sans-Nom."

"Sans-Nom?" Mrs Petty piped up. "Doesn't that mean 'no-name'?"

"That's right, for he's an orphan. I rescued him. He's been with me for many years, does four times the work of any of my other men."

"You're lucky to have such a good man in your employ. Be careful. A good European lad in these parts must be something of a prize. Somebody else may poach him."

De Locke scowled, shaking his head. "Nobody should dare to come near him," he said to Arthur Petty, as the rain started to pound on the tiled roof. "Alexandre's mine."

Chapter 3

DARTMOUTH AND BEYOND

Excitement and fear, Constance realized, were very similar. The flutter of birds' wings in her heart, the empty feeling in the arches of her feet, the thump of her pulse in her ears. Quietly, quietly, feeling around in the dark, she packed the smallest trunk she could find with clothes, books, apples and biscuits. It was midnight. Daphne lay sleeping in their soft bed, oblivious. Constance didn't want her cousin to be scolded for knowing about the midnight flight, so she said nothing. She had written a note, making herself sad at the thought of not seeing Daphne for many months.

It had all happened very quickly, in the end. She had expected Father to stay a number of weeks, as he usually did. But four days after his arrival, he had caught her on her way upstairs from the supper table, bidding her a solemn farewell.

"I won't see you in the morning, child. There is a favorable tide at five tomorrow morning, and a good wind. I will be heading away. I hope to find you well on my return."

That was the moment that the excitement and fear had surged to life inside her. She had to steel herself, put her half-formed plan into action.

Constance carefully closed the lid of the trunk, but she misjudged the fastenings in the dark. The snap of the buckles was unexpectedly loud. Daphne stirred. Constance froze. Silence and stillness returned. She laced on her bonnet and stood, hand reaching for the door.

"Constance?"

She spun.

Daphne sat up, drowsy, puzzled. "What on earth are you doing?"

Her voice was clear and piping in the quiet gloom, so Constance threw herself on the bed and pressed her hand to her cousin's lips.

"Shh," she said. "You'll wake the whole house."

"What time is it? What are you doing?" Daphne whispered when Constance set her lips free.

Constance fished the note from the front of her dress. "I was going to leave you this. . . ."

"Leave me . . . ? Are you going somewhere?"

Constance nodded, settling on her elbows next to Daphne. "To Ceylon."

Daphne's eyes widened as she guessed Constance's plan. "Oh, how very thrilling."

"You mustn't stop me. And you mustn't tell a soul."

"I won't stop you, Constance. But tomorrow morning at breakfast I will tell Mamma; for if I don't, she will worry extremely. By then, you will be gone."

Constance admitted that this was a good idea.

"How on earth will you get on board?"

"By the gangway, Daphne. It isn't hard to slip aboard unnoticed. Staying hidden is the challenge."

"But, cousin," Daphne continued, "how can you bear to travel so far by sea? Where will you sleep? In a dirty hammock under the deck, with no windows? There will be men everywhere, churls and drunkards. Knaves who have never seen a woman before. I shouldn't like to spend so long on a boat."

"It's not a *boat*, Daphne. It's a ship, or a barque, or even a vessel, but don't let a seaman hear you call it a *boat*." Constance laughed. "In any case, Father often takes on passengers, good families, many women. But he isn't this time because he's leaving in such a hurry. I'll stow away in one of the roundhouse cabins at the stern. I'll have windows. I know Father's ship well enough, I know many of his crew. I won't be in danger from them." Here she grimaced. "Just from Father when he finds out. I wonder if I can stay hidden all the way to Good Hope." She climbed off the bed and picked up the trunk. "I have to go. They're sailing in just under five hours. If I don't slip aboard now, it will be too busy later. Somebody will notice me."

Daphne threw back the covers and leapt up to hug Constance. "I shall miss you, cousin. But I am so very excited about your adventure."

With her free hand Constance stroked her cousin's hair, wishing she could be just a fraction quieter.

Daphne stood back, squeezed her hand. "I do hope you find your mother," she said softly.

Constance smiled, feeling the flutters again. She wondered if she had raised her expectations too high. But if Father felt confident enough to make this hastily arranged voyage to the east, with hardly any outgoing cargo—he would lose a great deal of money on the journey—then finding her mother must surely be a distinct possibility. "I hope so too, cousin," she said. "I have waited for her a very long time."

The early-morning air was chill, moist. Only starlight and a quarter moon lit her way across the cobbled quayside to *Good Bess*. Rain had come and gone, leaving puddles on the rutted ground. Above her, voices murmured softly on board; a light glowed in one of the portholes. The gangway waited. She stopped and placed her trunk at her feet, sticking to the shadows a few moments to catch her breath. What was she doing? She had never been further from home than London. Stars shone above her, Betelgeuse and Rigel anchoring the shape of Orion. Imaginings of the East pervaded her mind: broad sunlight, the smell of spices. Newly committed to her adventure, she bent to pick up her trunk. The buckle snapped open; the lid tumbled backwards, overbalancing it. Her apples rolled out and away, plopping into the water. Her clothes and biscuits landed in a muddy puddle.

She could have cried, this small setback too much for her at such a tense moment. She gathered what she could, leaving the biscuits for the rats. As quiet as she could, she headed up the gangway, then made her way aft to the roundhouse.

She had been aboard Father's ship numerous times, but was always shocked by the intensity of its unpleasant smell.

The lingering odors of tea, cinnamon and pepper were overwhelmed by the smell of mildew, salt, old fish, unwashed bodies. The smells were trapped by the claustrophobic spaces and had leeched into the wood. She ducked her head under the beams. There were cabins down here, usually reserved for paying travellers. Constance began trying doors in the dark. The first was locked. The next was not. She opened the cabin door and slipped inside.

The ceilings were low, and for a tall girl like Constance this would mean stooping under beams and hanging lanterns for the entire journey. She put her trunk at her feet and closed the door behind her. Darkness. She waited for her eyes to adjust, listening to her own breathing, feeling the almost imperceptible bob and sway of the ship, which, although not yet under sail, was still subject to the uncertain footing of water. She could make out shapes: heavy furniture that she knew would be lashed down. Moonlight waited outside the window. She moved towards it, striking her ankle on something hard, making her way around it—a table, she felt it with her hands—and then hitting her knees. Directly under the window was a bed. Not soft and welcoming like her bed at home— the first pang of homesickness—but long and narrow and flat with no linen. She lay down carefully. Her eyes had adapted now, and she gained a dim picture of the cabin. A sofa, a writing desk, a dresser, a chair, and a mirror. She turned her eyes to the window and listened.

Gradually, sounds began to gather. Footsteps on the gangway, voices calling to each other. Was that Father? She couldn't be sure. Shouting, laughing. Chickens clucking. The sky began to shed some of its ink. The movement and noise now grew frantic. Father's voice was strong and certain now, barking orders. Her anxiety swelled as she thought of him finding her. He couldn't find her, not yet. Not until they were well beyond English waters. She didn't want to be sent home.

Dawn drew near, the sky washed to pastel blue. Constance could see the detail in her cabin now, the scarred wood floor, the dusty age of the furniture, the faded Eastern rug.

More footsteps, running. She tensed, wondering if she should hide. But they scuttled past. The ship creaked, loosened from its stays.

And began to move.

Constance sat up, daring a glance out the window. The quayside slipped away from her, and she felt a sudden pang of vulnerability. If she felt this way less than twenty feet from the land, how on earth would she manage to make it all the way to Ceylon?

But then the wind caught the sails and she felt *Good Bess* heel to one side. The ship gathered speed, and a pleasant giddiness surprised her. Cutting through the water, *Good Bess* moved out towards the mouth of the river and the open sea. Constance liked the fluid motion, the silky movement as solidity fell away, almost like she imagined flying would be. The sky brightened; the first waves hit the bow, making a rhythmic splashing noise. They were on their way, and the thrill of excitement was more intense than the dull ache of homesickness.

Constance kneeled on the bed and watched as the land behind her lost its familiarity through distance, became nothing more than a dark outline on the horizon. A collection of rough-voiced gulls followed them, catching warm air under their wings and morning sunlight on top of them. She could hear her father's voice on the poop deck above her, but couldn't make out his words. He began to whistle, an old jig that he always whistled aimlessly when he was happy. What a strange way to discover something about her father: that sailing made him happy. She'd always assumed that he was a seaman because that was how he made money. The whistle faded away. She lay down on her bed and watched the lantern in the middle of the room sway back and forth on the gentle swell. Tiredness caught up with her, and her eyes fluttered closed.

Whistling. Very close.

She sat upright, heart thudding. Father. She scrambled onto the floor and behind the dresser. From here, she could see her trunk at the front of the room. If he opened the door, she would be discovered.

But he didn't open the door. The whistling continued. There were thumping and footfalls nearby. Constance turned her eyes to the wall, a thin partition between this cabin and the next.

Between her cabin and her father's.

She almost laughed. She had unwittingly taken the cabin next to his. In fact, she had tried his cabin door in the dark at midnight. What a blessing it had been locked! She climbed back onto the bed as quietly as a mouse. Silence would have to be her strongest ally over the coming days, for the bear slept close by and he was fearsome when angered.

———

Henry Blackchurch leaned on the rail, watching the wake of the ship. The silvery twilight had blackened the sea; the evening chill grew more intense. They had been the lucky recipients of favorable winds all day, and now, as they sailed into the first night of their journey, Henry had come to believe that it was some kind of sign from above. He was being sent good winds because his journey was fated: they would make quick time to Ceylon, they would find Faith, and she would return home with him.

Henry sighed, allowing himself a rare moment of melancholic reflection. In sixteen years, he had changed greatly. After frustrating results from the few leads he'd had, Henry had aged significantly, the wear of worry appropriate on his face. What would Faith think of him now? He knew instantly that this was his last chance.

"Sir, a moment please?"

Henry turned, straightening his spine. Jack Maitland, his first officer, stood there: a scrubbed potato of a man, altogether too serious for his young years.

"Yes, Maitland?"

"The crew have been asking if we'll stop at Porto Santo as usual. If the winds continue favorably, we should be there around a week from now."

Henry shook his head emphatically. "No. There isn't time to stop, it would slow us down. We'll go all the way to Good Hope, put ashore there for a short while."

"Good Hope? But there will be letters to send. . . ."

"If we see an English ship on her way home, we'll ask

her crew to take letters for us." He couldn't bear the idea of stopping. He wouldn't be able to breathe again until they saw the coast of India. Interminable pauses in the journey would squeeze his heart, make him itch.

Maitland nodded, then said tentatively, "Sir, why *are* we going to Ceylon? In such a hurry? With no trading stock aboard?"

"We are going because I said so," Henry answered irritably, recognizing the flimsiness of his excuse. Was it embarrassment that kept him from telling Maitland the truth? Or fear that if he began to tell the story, that they were searching for the most precious cargo of them all, his voice would catch and he would be revealed for the sentimental fool he really was?

"Aye, sir," Maitland said curtly.

Henry listened to him stride off, trying to recapture the pleasant feelings he had experienced before the conversation. They had dissolved with the last of the daylight, replaced instead with the uncertain dark.

———

Deep in the night, Constance woke.

She strained her ears. A noise had roused her, but all was silent now. She flipped over so she could see the sky through the window. The night was very clear, and she could see the tip of the Little Bear's tail, glowing icily. She had no pillows or blankets and had to make do with a rolled-up dress under her head, a long coat and an extra pair of stockings. Despite the lack of home comforts, she found herself very comfortable. The constant motion of the sea rocked her, and she began to drift back to sleep almost immediately.

Then the noise again. Like wood being roughly sawn. Her eyes blinked open. It was Father snoring.

She drifted in and out of sleep, the snores periodically waking her. Then came the pains in her stomach . . . hunger pains.

Gradually they became too much to sleep through. The sky was still dark, but she could sense light gathering somewhere nearby. If she was going to slip to the pantry, now was the time. If only her food hadn't spilled out at the quay.

She sat up, determined to make it unnoticed to the pantry and back. But as soon as she sat up, a great wave of nausea broke over her. She lay down again. In a second, the feeling went away. Slowly she rose for a second time, this time making it to her feet. She took a deep breath. Not too bad.

One foot in front of the other. The sea rolled; her

stomach rolled with it. She swallowed hard. All she needed was to get to the pantry, steal some food, then make it back here to her bed. But being upright was proving difficult. She moved to the cabin door, opened it quietly, and listened hard. Nothing. Shuffling forward quietly, her stomach gurgling dizzily, she made her way amidships. Through the main deck steerage, ducking under beams, past a long scarred table. The smell of food gone cold hung in the air. Old trunks were stacked against the wall, a dirt-streaked cannon lashed down beside them. She could see the sky through the windows above. But there was no other light or air, and the nausea swelled inside her.

Finally she was at the pantry door. It was locked.

Tears threatened, and Constance let them squeeze out quietly. She could no longer tell if the pains in her stomach were from hunger or sickness, so she hurried back to her cabin as quietly as she could and lay down. The feeling abated slightly.

Then it rushed upon her suddenly. She climbed up to kneel on her bed, thrust open the window and, shuddering down to her knees, threw up into the vast ocean. Retch after retch, sweat prickling her face, huge acidic waves of it poured out of her.

Afterward, she sat down, wiping her damp face on the

hem of her dress. The shudders started again inside her, so she lay on her back, willing them to subside. They did, but not fully. Father snored on, and Constance curled on her side in the dim room, breathing softly and clutching her bilious stomach.

Day broke, the wind picked up, the sea grew rougher. At least Father wasn't in his cabin any more so she needn't vomit quietly. Every hour or so, she had to put her face to the window and throw up. She tried to drink a little water from the decanter on the table. But then the ship heeled sharply starboard without warning, and the water spilled all over the floor. Hunger made her weak; sickness made her weaker. As the sea grew rougher, it seemed that everything was in motion around her. The lantern swung, the furniture shifted an inch this way and that on its ropes, her trunk skated the floor and back again. Her eyes grew dizzy; she longed for stillness. It was time to be sick again.

This time the wind had changed, now blowing briskly across the stern of the ship. She didn't notice, and when she threw up, the wind carried it all back into her face, her hair, and over her bodice.

She climbed down from the bed, holding back sobs. She struggled out of her dress and wiped her face on it.

The sour smell of sickness was everywhere. Her hands were shaking, and her face felt cold and sweaty all at once. She collapsed onto the bed, wishing she had never set foot on *Good Bess*.

Henry sat down to dinner in the cuddy dining saloon, well pleased with their progress. Only two and a half days at sea and they had already cleared the Scilly Islands and were making fast pace towards the Bay of Biscay. Old Harry, the cook, was so used to life at sea that, despite his crippled left leg, he stuck to the deck as though nailed, even in the most tempestuous of conditions. He plopped down a roasted chicken that swam in its juices on a pewter plate. Potatoes skidded along next to it.

Matthew Burchfield, the ship's surgeon, peered over his spectacles at the meal.

"Jus' killed today," Old Harry said.

"Quite," Burchfield replied.

Henry was glad to see Burchfield and Maitland on time for dinner, but Hickey, the second officer, was late as usual.

"We'll start without Hickey," Henry said, picking up the carving knife. "Maitland, I'll need you to have a word with him. I like to run a tight ship, and—

The door slammed open. The ship rolled. Henry looked around startled.

In the threshold, white as a sheet and wearing a filthy stained dress, was his daughter Constance.

"What the blazes?"

"Father, I'm . . ." she gasped, before collapsing in a heap on the deck.

Chapter 4

FROM THE BAY OF BISCAY

In the days that followed, Constance suffered a fever that turned her thoughts into a confused, nightmarish fog. Imagined spiders gathered in the corners of her cabin, old tales of Indian gods and goddesses wove themselves into dreams of jungles and fires, a growling bearded monster—not unlike her father—waited behind her eyelids if she dared to sleep. She called for Aunty Violet, disoriented and frightened. In rare lucid moments, she was aware of a thin man with spectacles, the ship's surgeon, who attended her carefully, if coldly. Father came once; he barked questions at her but was removed by the doctor when she started to cry. After that she slid back into her jungle dreams and didn't emerge for what seemed like weeks.

In fact, it was only two days later that the fever broke, and she woke feeling weak but comfortable. She was alone in her cabin. Somebody had brought her sheets and a duck-down pillow. She still wore her dirty dress, and the smell of vomit hung sourly about her. On the table a decanter stood, with a cup next to it. Water. She smacked her lips together, pulled back the sheet and rose slowly.

The nausea was gone. Good.

The ship rolled underneath her; she caught herself on the back of the chair. The door opened, and the thin man came in.

"Back to your bed," he ordered.

She scurried back to bed, pulling her sheets up again. He filled a cup with water and brought it to her. As she drank, he stared at her with flinty grey eyes.

"Thank you," she said meekly.

"I am Matthew Burchfield, the ship's surgeon."

"I know. We've met before. When I was just a child."

"You are still a child," he said, with condescending amusement.

The water tasted sweet. Her stomach rumbled with hunger.

"How long have I been seasick?" she asked.

"You've been abed two days. But you weren't seasick. Perhaps initially that's all it was, but you've had a fever, quite a serious one. Your father has been very worried."

Constance almost laughed. Her father saw her for a dozen days in every year. If she died, he'd barely notice.

"Mr. Burchfield," she said hesitantly. "I wonder if I might . . . eat something?"

He lifted his eyes in a world-weary expression and sighed deeply. "I shall speak to Old Harry." He moved to the cabin door, and his nostrils twitched. "When you are feeling strong enough, I'll find you a bar of marine soap and a tub of seawater to wash your clothes."

As soon as he was gone, Constance rose and went to her trunk. She pulled out one of the other dresses: a short-sleeved muslin dress with a satin ribbon. It was splattered with mud, but at least it didn't stink. She quickly changed, then returned to her bed. The little effort required had exhausted her.

A brief knock at the door. She assumed it was Old Harry with her food, but before she could call, "Come in," her father strode in, thunderclouds on his eyebrows.

"Father," she yelped, pulling the sheets up defensively.

"Constance," he replied sternly, sitting himself on the chair next to the table and folding his arms across his chest. "You are well, then?"

"Still weak," she replied. "And very hungry."

"So I hear. My crew are, at this moment, running about

trying to find food for you. When they should be doing other things."

Constance opened her mouth to say, "I'm sorry," but sensed it was too early. He would give her much more to apologize for yet.

He stood and began to pace. As he did so, a small glass object fell from his pocket. He didn't notice, and she didn't mention it, bracing herself for the onslaught.

"What on earth were you thinking?" he said angrily. "You have caused me untold embarrassment and inconvenience."

"I wanted to come with you to find Mother," she said simply, in case he had forgotten that she had overheard the original conversation.

"That much is clear. But your desires are not the only engine driving the globe, Constance. You should have stayed at home, as any dutiful daughter would, and waited for news from me. Instead, you have followed your silly impulses and within an eye's blink created pandemonium on my ship. The crew are laughing at me behind my back. What a great joke: Henry Blackchurch can control a crew of eighteen sea dogs, but he can't control his daughter. I had thought you an intelligent girl, Constance. But only a selfish ninny would act as you have."

Constance dropped her head forward so he wouldn't see the tears pricking her eyes.

"Well you might hang your head in shame, girl. So, you are aboard now and, as you no doubt reckoned, I'm not turning back. Who knows how long it could delay me?"

She didn't know whether to feel relieved by this knowledge or not.

He stopped pacing next to her bed. "Here are the rules that you will now follow. You will be invisible. Stay in here. Do not come near the cuddy saloon or the great cabin. I will ensure meals are brought to you twice a day. Every evening, you may take a turn about the poop deck for your health. But keep away from my crew, do not speak to them, do not ask them questions. God willing, they will forget you are even here. If you need anything, you speak to me directly." He nodded, once, definitively. It was her cue to speak.

She lifted her head. "Yes, Father," she said. "I am truly sorry for—"

"Silence! You are not sorry. You are glad you did it, and you would do it the same again," he said.

He was right, and although her mouth moved to deny it, her heart wouldn't let her.

"Yes, I thought so." He turned on his heel, striding towards the door again. "Food will arrive soon. Burchfield recommends another day in bed. I think some fresh air up on deck this evening might do you good. I expect you will make up your own mind."

The door slammed behind him, shaking the thin walls. Constance lay back on the soft pillow, telling herself to be brave. He would have found her out eventually, and he wasn't sending her home or—worse—putting her off with some dreadful acquaintance in a foreign country. Yes, he was angry, but his displeasure wasn't such a mighty thing to be feared: it wasn't as though he ever took pleasure in his daughter's company after all.

She turned; the shining object caught her eye. She flipped back the sheets and bent to pick it up. A brass and glass compass, small enough to sit in the hollow of her palm. She rolled it over in her hands. Tiny words were engraved on the base. She took it to the window, so the light could make the inscription clear. Her heart picked up a beat. She knew it would be from her mother, a message of love: *come and find me*.

It wasn't. It was from Violet, his sister. *A safe return always, V.*

Disappointed, she took the compass to the cabin door

and made to follow her father. Voices within stopped her. She remembered her father's warning, that she must be invisible. Instead, she slipped into his cabin and placed it on the dresser.

As she was leaving, she noticed Father's bed. No pillow, no linen. She felt mingled guilt and surprise. Her pillow and sheets had not come out of storage: there was little room to store such things on a ship. He had given her his own.

———————

It was a clear night, cool but not cold. *Good Bess* carved through the waves resolutely, a strong north-westerly hard against her sails. Henry stood on the quarterdeck with Maitland at the wheel, gazing up the mighty mast.

"We've been blessed by good winds," Maitland said, reading his mind.

"Somebody up there likes me," Henry joked gruffly.

"I was thinking it was a pity that we had no cargo to trade. It might have been our most lucrative journey ever." Maitland forced a smile, twitching his moustache up at the corners. "That's not a criticism of your motives, Captain."

"I know." But Henry was not unaware of the discontent that laced Maitland's words.

He grew irritated, dropping his voice to a harsh whisper. "Loose talk like that won't do, Maitland," he continued. "The crew aren't saying such things, are they? I hope nobody has forgotten that my daughter is aboard." He hooked his thumb over his shoulder and Maitland glanced up to the poop deck, where Constance sat on a chicken coop, star-gazing.

Maitland cringed. "Sorry, Captain. I didn't know she was there."

Henry was bemused by this statement. Constance had been told to become invisible, and she had achieved this admirably. Days could pass without him seeing her. Old Harry left meals at her cabin twice a day. Henry had no idea what she amused herself with down there. He had given her what books he could find, but there was little room on a merchantman for reading material.

For the last two weeks, with Constance aboard, he had been in a state of persistent anxiety. His thoughts were scattered, making him short-tempered with his crew. His daughter would never guess how much vexation she had caused him. All it would take was one idle conversation, between her and one loose-lipped sailor, and everything would come undone. Each party had secrets about him that he wanted to keep from the other. He was afraid of being exposed both as a sentimental fool and as a flint-eyed scoundrel. That all of it was Faith's fault was a detail not lost on him.

A crosswind flapped the sails. Sensing the change, Maitland gave a softly uttered order to harden up all sheets to keep *Good Bess* sailing at best speed. Henry turned and made his way aft and up the ladder to the poop deck. The rush of the water masked his footfalls. Constance, still gazing at the constellations, hadn't heard him. He paused, watching her a moment. Much had been made of how closely she resembled him: her eyes and hair, her skin, the slight flair of her nostrils, the upward tilt of her eyebrows. But Faith was there too: the proud uprightness of her back, the grace of her movements, the gestures of her hands. Aspects of her mother that Constance had never seen or couldn't remember, but which had been passed to her through blood.

Constance turned. Her eyes widened as she saw him, but she didn't smile. Nor did he. She probably suspected that he was a bear, an ogre, a villain. Yes, he was all these things, and so it was better for both of them if they had little to do with each other. He nodded once, then made his way back down the ladder without a word.

As their journey progressed, Constance's cabin began to grow warm and stuffy during the day. She was at the window, trying to gulp the air, when her door opened without a knock. She looked up. Walter, the ship's boy, stood hesitantly in the threshold, a hessian sack at his feet.

"You ought to have knocked," she said.

He stared at her, wordlessly.

"Can I help?" she asked. It was odd—extremely odd—for one of Father's crew to be here in her cabin.

"I . . . ah. Sorry, miss. It's just we seen a ship, miss, an English ship on her way home. Cap'n said I was to ask all aboard if they had any letters to go back wiv her." He removed his hat and scratched his mousy hair. "But now I'm not sure if I was supposed to ask you as well."

Constance deduced from this that the crew of *Good Bess* had been told to stay away from her, just as she had been told to stay away from them.

"I do have a letter," she said, thinking of the pages and pages she had written for Daphne. "But it might take me a moment to finish it and address it."

"The ship's close, miss. There's not much time. And . . . only, I can't wait, like. I think I should . . . go." He kicked the hessian sack towards her. "When you've written your letter, put it in there and leave the sack outside your door."

"Good idea, Walter. Thank you."

He retreated, and she quickly sat up at her writing desk and scratched a few hasty lines to end the letter. She folded it and sealed it, then opened the bag to slip it in. Lying on top of the mail was a letter addressed to Aunty Violet.

Cautiously, Constance plucked the letter from the bag and turned it over. She knew it was written by Father, and wondered what he had written about her. She wished her eyes could see through paper, for she had no intention of actually opening the letter. But then the door to her cabin opened again and Father stood there. She hastily tucked his letter to Violet in her skirts, lest he discover her examining it.

"Has that fool Walter been bothering you?"

"Not at all. He just let me know I could send a letter home."

Father clicked his fingers. "Hand me the mail bag. I shall take it. We are going to parley with this ship, see if they'll take these to England."

Constance handed him the bag, while his letter to Violet seemed to burn a hole in her dress. What was she to do? Pull it out now and let him think she intended to open it? Or keep it hidden and know it would never get to its destination?

"You stay down here," Father continued. "You should be able to see her from your window. A pretty vessel. Looks like a whaler; her copper sheathing is torn. Probably from ice in the Southern Ocean."

Self-preservation won out. There were many ways a letter could go missing between here and Dartmouth. She wouldn't necessarily be blamed. Even if she was, it would be a long time in the future. She moved slightly, pushing the letter further out of view.

He turned and left, closing the door behind him. She pulled her trunk in front of the door so nobody else could burst in uninvited, and climbed onto her bed under the window.

The whaler was a London ship that had been out at sea for nearly two years in icy waters. Her head had been brought up to the wind, her sun-stained head sails flapping hard. Father and the whaler's captain communicated first through their speaking trumpets, then a rowboat was sent between the vessels to transfer the letters.

Constance watched the transaction from her window, longing to be up on deck in the sun and fresh air, rather than cooped up here like a guilty secret.

Eventually, the two ships went their separate ways, and Constance's thoughts turned to how best to dispose of Father's letter. She decided to wait until night-time and let it fly out her window on the wind. That left her three or four hours with the letter, her fingers itching to pick off the seal. Was there any way at all she could resist it? She knew the letter would mention her, expose his feelings about her stowing away. Perhaps it might even mention further news of her mother.

The last thought decided it for her. She had already stolen the letter; she might as well complete the sin by reading it. She unfolded the crisp sheets and leaned towards the light of the window to read.

Dear Sister,
As you have no doubt heard by now, Constance is
aboard with me. I expect that Daphne was aware of
these plans and probably had a hand in devising them,
and I hope that you have punished her accordingly.

Constance clenched her fists, thinking about Daphne getting in trouble on her behalf. Then she remembered that the letter would never reach its destination.

While the girl's presence on board is extraordinarily vexing, I expect it will be easier when we reach Nagakodi. William Howlett, whom I will stay with, has a daughter her age, and they can entertain each other with their silliness and leave me in peace.

Again she bristled. Leave him in peace? She'd spoken less than a hundred words to him since her illness. She had taken his directives very seriously and isolated herself. And did he really think that she would be satisfied to entertain herself with some silly girl when she hoped to help him find her mother? Clearly he thought her still a child.

I am full of doubts, Violet. You know that I cannot speak of these things in your company, but I find it easier to write them down. I am terribly afraid that I won't find her. I cannot imagine how Faith might have spent the last sixteen years, if she tried to get back to us, if she has been treated unkindly. But then, I am equally afraid that I will find her. Much has transpired since her disappearance. You know what I did, and you have forgiven me. But will she? I am, perhaps, not the man I once was. When she vanished, something became cold and brittle inside me. It explains what I did, but does not excuse it.

Constance scanned the rest of the letter, but it was only information about winds and tides, and the ports they had passed but not stopped at. She lay down on her bed, holding the letter against her chest, puzzled. *You know what I did, and you have forgiven me.* She had no idea at all what her father meant, but it stirred uneasiness deep inside her.

What *had* Father done?

Chapter 5

TUMKOTTAI, SOUTHERN INDIA

De Locke had never paid Alexandre with money. He gave him a place to sleep on *La Reine des Perles*, and he gave him plenty of food, books and drawing materials that he picked up on his regular trips to Tuticorin. The lad wanted for nothing—he was strong, healthy, well-rested, and lived in paradise. But, rarely, de Locke had moments of niggling worry. Alexandre was different. There was a softness in him that shouldn't be there, not after the life he had lived. Certainly, he was fearless and tough. De Locke had never once seen him shrink from a task, no matter how strenuous or messy. But he had dreams in his eyes. Dreams could be dangerous.

De Locke watched Alexandre as the boy sketched, settled atop a soft mound of sand. Alexandre worked slowly and carefully, hardly looking up. De Locke became curious. What was he drawing?

He tucked his pistol in his waistband and followed the stone stairs down to the grass verge, and then to the beach.

A gust of wind peppered his face with sand, rattled at his shirt. Alexandre hadn't yet noticed him. Thunder again, low and distant. Alexandre looked up and saw de Locke approaching.

He fumbled with his drawing book. Pages flapped. He dropped his charcoals. He had all his papers under his control by the time de Locke had crouched next to him, but de Locke had the distinct impression that Alexandre had hidden something from him.

"What are you drawing, boy?"

Alexandre showed him a picture of palm trees, the sea stretched behind them, *La Reine des Perles* rendered in fine detail.

"That's very good work, Alexandre. Perhaps we should frame it and sell it at the markets."

Alexandre lifted his shoulders, a gesture that de Locke suspected was full of fake casualness. "If you like."

"It was a joke, boy. But if we have many more days of poor weather, we might have to resort to selling a pearl diver's sketches." De Locke liked to pretend that he had little money, that they were always one pearl away from poverty. He wondered, now, whether Alexandre believed him. He had a servant; countless items of finely carved furniture; a whitewashed villa made exotic by Indian colonnades, stone lions on the gate posts, forebodingly dark teak doors. De Locke couldn't take his eyes off Alexandre's drawing book. What had he hidden? Plans to cut his master's throat and steal his riches?

A few drops of rain fell.

"Come inside, boy," de Locke said. "It's almost two. You may dine with me today."

Puzzled surprise lit Alexandre's eyes; he nodded eagerly. De Locke led him back up the beach and into the villa. Mari, his servant, was busy in the kitchen, and the smell of spices and bubbling cream filled the air. Since she had been cooking for him, he had outgrown his waistband twice. His too-small clothes now took up a quarter of his hanging space.

He stopped in the dining room and Alexandre stopped behind him, dropped his book on the table and moved to pull out a dining chair.

"Wait, boy. You know you can't dine shirtless." He indicated with a tilt of his head. "Go to my wardrobe and find yourself a shirt."

"Yes, Gilbert," Alexandre answered, dutifully moving off.

As soon as Alexandre was out of the room, de Locke

pounced on his drawing book. There were many sketches of *La Reine des Perles*, very detailed, fine rigging lines carefully itemized. At the back, he found the drawing Alexandre had hidden. It was completely different from the others. The misty spire of a church, on the far side of a wide field. A stormy sky, leaves whirling across the page. This was not India. This was not the paradise Alexandre lived in. This was Europe. The cool, almost detached, fineness was gone. Warmth, longing, had been fused into the lines. He turned the page. The same scene again, this time under a still, cloudless sky, sunlight on the church's windows. And then another, and another. In all, he found twelve drawings of the same scene. Footsteps in the hallway made him drop the book hastily. He turned. It was only Mari, bringing bowls of steaming rice to the table. He moved to the window recess, leaning his hands on the cool stone sill.

De Locke knew what the drawings meant. Alexandre was longing for home, for France, for *somewhere else*. But how could he long for a place where he had known such unhappiness? De Locke had always assumed his lack of family or friends had allowed Alexandre to cut off from his home. Instead, he had developed an attachment to this place that he kept imagining.

Alexandre was indispensable. If he was homesick, that meant he might run off. De Locke couldn't have that. So what was he to do? Offer him money, a share of the profits? The thought caused a pain to shoot through his guts. He pressed his hands over his navel.

"Gilbert?" Alexandre had entered the room silently and stood at the dining table in a shirt too short for him.

De Locke forced a smile. "Sit, boy," he said. "Eat."

Mari kept bringing food as well as strong wine that Alexandre refused. The meal progressed and de Locke drank too much; his head felt dull and heavy. Finally, he couldn't hold his tongue still any longer.

"Do you ever think about France, boy?"

Alexandre answered immediately. "Not much. You?"

"There's nothing there for me. The cold, the crowds. It's a stale place."

"Is that why you left?"

It occurred to de Locke, brightly and sharply, that telling Alexandre the real reason he left could be very persuasive. He had never told anybody before, but the good dose of claret and the desperation to keep Alexandre drove him forward. His heart sped a little, the old guilt making his words tumble out fast.

"It was in the little town of Buis. Do you remember it?"

Alexandre shook his head.

"It's where I found you."

"Oh," Alexandre said. "I never went into the town. We camped in the fields."

"I was visiting friends. They brought me to Givot's show, and that's where I first saw you. I'd been in the pearling trade for ten years already, but I usually came home to France in between journeys. After the show, my friends and I all wandered into town. We found a coffee house, we drank coffee, but I wanted something . . . stronger." He raised his glass to show what he meant. "My friends and I parted. I fell in with a group sharing rum in a back room. I don't even remember their names now. Our conversations turned into friendly arguments. The proprietor of the coffee shop asked us to leave. We continued our discussions in the street."

De Locke shivered as he remembered the details. The narrow, cobbled alley. The smell of damp evening, of rotting garbage. Their voices echoing between the buildings as lamps were extinguished and the emptiness after midnight engulfed them. "One by one, they left for their homes. Until I was left with one fellow, a big man with all his front teeth missing. Friendly arguments became heated. I said something—I don't even remember it now—and he took offense." He found his voice stuck in his throat now. "He seized me—I thought he would crush me. He wouldn't let me go." He remembered the suffocating smell of him, feeling like a bird in a bear's embrace. "I still don't know what he intended, because he was laughing. But I was . . . ." Afraid: he had been desperately afraid, had cried for his mama, had wet his breeches. But he couldn't let Alexandre know that fear had motivated him. "I was insulted. How dare he? I carried a pistol at my waistband; I still do." He lifted the flap of his jacket so Alexandre could see it. "I pulled it out, pressed it into his chest, and pulled the trigger."

Alexandre had paused, a spoon frozen halfway to his mouth.

De Locke smiled coldly.

"Did you . . . kill him?"

"I did. Such a lot of blood." He swirled his wine in his glass, then forced a bright tone. "Then I ran back to Givot's show, found you. We sailed, as you'll remember, the next day. I will never go back, for I do not wish to face a murderer's punishment."

Alexandre kept eating, his expression giving nothing away.

De Locke leaned towards him. "You see, that is what happens to those who cross me, boy. I am not a man to make angry. Especially in these lawless parts. Why, imagine if I got it in my head to shoot you? Who would know? Who would care?"

Whatever Alexandre was feeling, he had now become adept at hiding it. "I expect you're right," he said. "But I trust you are pleased enough with me not to shoot me."

De Locke leaned back in his chair and laughed, dizzy drunkenness making his head spin. "I am well pleased with you, boy. If you continue to serve me well, we will continue to get along."

Alexandre finished his meal, then stood. "Thank you for inviting me to dine."

"Stay a little longer. Have some wine."

"No thank you. It makes me sick. I have some jobs to do aboard." He began to untie the shirt he wore, but de Locke held up his hand.

"No, no. You keep it. It doesn't fit me any more."

"Thank you, Gilbert."

De Locke watched him go, a sense of warm satisfaction in his stomach. Alexandre wouldn't go now. De Locke had scared him good.

Under the bubbling silence of the water, Alexandre could hear his heartbeat. Steady, strong. With his pick, he collected oysters, the straps of his gunnysack threatening to float away. His companion divers ran out of breath and went up. Alexandre watched, made sure he was alone, and began to crack the oysters open.

Nothing. Nothing. Nothing.

In the weeks since de Locke had confessed to murder, Alexandre had tried not to become too desperate to get away. He had never particularly liked his master, but the threat—for certainly de Locke was trying to threaten him—had driven out of his heart the last shred of loyalty. Alexandre was only nineteen. Years stretched ahead of him. He wouldn't spend them with de Locke, and he couldn't allow de Locke to cut them short in a fit of temper either.

So his fingers worked swiftly. Too swiftly. He cut his hand on the sharp edge of a shell. Blood smoked into the water. His heart picked up. These waters regularly played host to sharks, and blood was like a beacon to them. Still, he kept opening oysters. His breath was growing hard in his lungs; it would soon be time to pull the rope, signal that he had to come up.

Nothing. Nothing. Nothing.

Then . . .

He almost didn't see it, so used to the empty insides of oysters was he. But there it sat, gleaming softly. Small, but perfect. A symbol of purity and, for Alexandre, freedom.

A pearl.

Alexandre almost forgot himself and took a breath. But he didn't want the ocean to rush into his lungs. He quickly realized he hadn't thought this through. There was nowhere to hide the pearl. The gunnysack would be emptied on the deck, and his knee-length trousers had no pockets. A shadow above told him the other divers were descending again.

With his index finger, he pushed the pearl into his mouth and tucked it against his cheek with his tongue. Alexandre never spoke much; de Locke wouldn't notice if he stayed particularly quiet today. He pulled on the rope, his heart singing.

———

Later that evening, after the day's work was done, Alexandre split open the seam of his hammock with a knife and pushed the pearl inside it. Then he climbed into the hammock, and stopped for a while to reflect.

He and the two Sinhalese men had cracked open every oyster on the deck of *La Reine des Perles*, while de Locke looked on hungrily. No pearls today, which made Alexandre's deception all the more acute.

But Alexandre felt no guilt. He had not thieved from de Locke, he had thieved from the ocean. No, it wasn't theft. The ocean had offered him the pearl; he knew it. He had always respected her, loved her in his own way. Now she was ready to let him go.

All he needed was a ship to take him home. He would not be hasty. He would wait for another bout of bad weather, disappear before de Locke knew he was missing, make his way somehow to Tuticorin. And from there, France.

He climbed out of his hammock, found his drawing book—abandoned for weeks since de Locke's threat—and flipped to his favorite drawings.

But they were all muddled. September came before March, December's corner was bent. Somebody had been through these drawings.

De Locke, of course. A timely reminder that his master was not above searching his belongings.

Alexandre returned to his hammock, squeezed the pearl out of the seam and put it back in his mouth. It sat gently against his cheek. It would have to stay there until it was time to barter it for a passage home.

Chapter 6

THE CAPE OF GOOD HOPE

As *Good Bess* moved closer to the equator, that line around the centre of the world that the sun loved so dearly, it grew warmer and more oppressive in Constance's cabin. The wind was brisk, but blew in the wrong direction to flood through her windows. The low ceilings compounded the feeling of unbearable closeness, and her breath seemed woolly and hot in her lungs. The tedium of the journey, too, had begun to grind her down. At one stage, she saw another ship, but it steered to the east and soon disappeared, probably for Cape de Verd or the coast of Africa. Apart from that, and the occasional excitement of seeing flying fish, she grew fatigued by her own company. She read her astronomy books and worked her way through a complete edition of Shakespeare that Father had aboard. The thrill of adventure had long been replaced by boredom. How she longed for Daphne's bright company, for somebody to speak to. She supposed she could have spoken to her father, but he was all but a stranger to her. The closer she drew to adulthood, the less they could find in common. What would she say to him? What could they talk about that wouldn't lead to his chastising her in some way?

Old Harry, the cook who brought her two meals a day, was kind enough to speak a few words to her, though she was cautious not to ask for too much. He gave her all the important information: where they were, how the journey was progressing. They passed within twenty miles of Palma and then the peak of Tenerrife, but haze and thick clouds prevented her from seeing either. Once they moved into the path of the trade winds, their good speed was consolidated and their captain—her father— was reported to be mightily pleased with their progress. Without Harry's updates, she would have believed herself adrift in the ocean forever, not drawing any closer to land, just rolling and rolling on the endless waves.

One overcast afternoon shortly after they crossed to the other side of the world, it grew so hot in her cabin that she felt she couldn't breathe. It had rained that morning, and then the grey clouds had hung over them like a woollen blanket, trapping the moist heat. Her body grew sticky, uncomfortable. She couldn't bear to sit on her bed, because sweat gathered on the backs of her legs and trickled down behind her knees. She hung at her window, but caught none of the freshness in the breeze. She began to feel anxious, overwhelmed. Air, she needed air. But Father had told her, very forcefully, that she wasn't to leave her room during the day.

Well, then. She would just have to make sure her father didn't find out.

It was a big ship; there were only eighteen crew. Surely she could work her way up on deck, hide somewhere . . . The poop deck was out of the question: Father spent most of his time up there. The quarterdeck had plenty of places to hide, but saw most of the action. But the forecastle deck, right at the very front of the ship, would certainly catch the best breezes, and it would be safe.

Constance moved to the door, cracked it open and listened. There was nobody in the narrow corridor that led to the pantry. She scurried out, making her way quickly towards the root of the main mast. Here she paused, back pressed up against the round, smooth wood. The sour smell of the ship was strong in the airless space. Above, she could hear a commotion. Laughing, shouting. She kept moving. Then somebody called out, "All hands on deck." Footsteps everywhere. She crouched beside one of the eighteen-pound cannons, wriggling up against the wall. Her heart thudded dully as the sound of everybody moving surrounded her. Men dashed past, up the ladders onto the quarterdeck. They were in a hurry; they didn't have time to see a girl hiding in the shadows.

When Constance was sure everybody had passed, she rose and made for the ladder, curious, now, about the commotion. Carefully, she peeked out at the quarterdeck. She didn't have a clear line of sight; masts and ropes and the shadows of the sails were in the way. But now she could hear a loud clucking noise, flapping wings. She glimpsed men chasing about, laughing. Old Harry shouted instructions. It seemed he had gone to get chickens for dinner, and one had escaped. Guilt crept over her. Perhaps, like her, the chicken just wanted to feel the breeze. She mentally vowed not to eat chicken that afternoon.

Still, while they were all occupied with their game, they wouldn't see her creep up onto the forecastle deck. She hurried up, stepping around neatly coiled ropes, and found herself a place in front of the forecastle mast. The long bowsprit pointed out to sea before her, its rigging criss-crossed against the lowering sky. She sat, already blessing the wind, which tangled her hair behind her and cooled her sticky skin.

The ocean disappeared beneath her, grey and vast. She could taste salt on her lips. She closed her eyes and breathed deeply, freed from the oppression of her cabin. Voices nearby had her jerking upright, looking around. But they were coming from beneath her, through the wooden lattice that let light in to the spaces below. She remembered, then, that under the forecastle deck was where the skilled crew—boatswains, gunners and carpenters—had their accommodation.

"She certainly gave Old Harry a run," the first voice said gruffly.

"I think he'll relish carving her up," his companion replied in a thick Irish accent.

Laughter. She relaxed. They didn't know she was here.

Their conversation moved on, Gruff-voice and the Irishman. An albatross circled above, and she watched it, trying not to listen to them speak. They used the most unsavoury turn of phrase, and when she realized they were talking about a woman . . . and then a particular kind of woman . . . she was scandalized and curious all at once.

Eventually, though, they turned to other matters.

"So why do you think the captain is bringing us all this way without a cargo aboard?" said Gruff-voice.

"I reckon he's got something mighty precious waiting at the other end. An opportunity he had to chase quickly."

Constance smiled to herself. He was right, in a way. Her father did seek something precious, but it wouldn't earn him any money.

The Irishman continued. "Some of the others disagree with me. They say he's on the run, had to leave England in a hurry."

"In trouble? No, not Captain Blackchurch."

"You don't know then?" His voice dropped. "About his past?"

Constance's spine stiffened. She strained to hear every word.

"That rubbish," snorted Gruff-voice. "Piracy off the coast of Madagascar? I don't believe it."

"You don't, eh? Ask Old Harry sometime—he was there. The only crew member Cap'n Blackchurch has kept. The others he got rid of; they knew his dark secret. Cleaned himself up, hoisted the red duster instead of the Jolly Roger, and now he's respectable Henry Blackchurch Esquire. But I reckon at night he can still smell the blood on his hands."

Then they were gone. Constance was numb. Could it be true? Could Father be a pirate? A thief? A murderer? She realized she hardly knew anything about him, had spent so little time in his company. Now the question seemed obvious. What kind of man was her father?

In her cabin, alone, Constance had too much time to contemplate this question. Her suspicions, with nobody rational to help dispel them, multiplied until her mind teemed with them, and her feelings for her father iced over with fear, as though she were a character in one of Daphne's silly books. If only Father hadn't confessed to some horrible deed in the letter to Violet, she might have been able to dismiss these feelings. She had always taken pride in her rationality. Reason was a thing to be cherished, or so Dr. Poole said. But now, every time she saw Old Harry, all her veins and nerves lit up with the desire to ask him if the tale about her father were true. It took all her energy to hold the questions in. If it got back to Father that she knew his secret, he would be angry. And she was more afraid of that anger than ever.

A sudden change in wind direction blew the heat away, replacing it with the chill of the Southern Ocean. In the following days they suffered through heavy squalls, and

Constance no longer took her evening turn about the poop deck. Rather, she hunkered down in her cabin with her dread and wished with all her might that she was at home in England.

Then, one night, she had a nightmare. Father, with his clothes alight, roaring: a monster, a demon, brandishing two pistols like an old engraving she had seen of Blackbeard. One was pointed at her.

She woke. The room was filled with morning light. Somebody was knocking at her door. Alarmed, she pulled the blankets up to her chin.

Another soft knock. "Miss Constance?" It was Old Harry, with her breakfast.

"Come in." She had slept late. Usually she was up and dressed by now, sitting at her writing desk working on a letter to Daphne that enumerated every fear she felt about Father.

He brought her a tray with warm oats and honey on it, placing it on the little table in the centre of the room.

"Good weather has returned today, miss," he said as he straightened his back. "Our head is now right for the Cape; we've only twenty-eight degrees of longitude to run down. The captain says we'll stop there a few days. You'll be able to post your letter."

At mention of the captain, Constance felt the terror of her dream return to her. She couldn't help herself letting free a little groan of fear.

"What's wrong, miss? You've gone quite pale. Do you want me to call the surgeon?"

"No, no. I'm . . . I'll be fine." She forced a smile. "Harry, is my father . . . he's a good man, yes?"

"Why yes, of course."

"You've known him a long time."

"I've been with him for twenty years. Since my leg worked proper."

"Has he always been so? A good man, I mean?"

To Constance's horror, Harry's eyes flickered. He took a moment—it seemed an eternity—to answer her. And in that moment she knew, she *knew*. The Irishman had been telling the truth.

"He has always been as he is, miss," Harry said firmly. "The best captain I could have wished for."

"Of course." She tried to smile, but couldn't quite manage it. Harry wouldn't meet her eye; he left the room quietly. And from then on he told her nothing more about their journey, but delivered her meals wordlessly.

His silence told her everything she needed to know.

A week later, they caught their first glimpse of the Cape of Good Hope. It was midday, the sun hung vertical in the sky, and the clouds were nowhere in sight. Slowly, they made their way towards Table Bay. It was two in the morning when Constance woke to hear voices cheering; they had cast anchor. She kneeled up to her window and saw Table Mountain, its long flat peak ghostly in the clear moonlight.

"Africa," she murmured. And the incredible thought that she would soon set her feet on that mysterious continent caused a thrill to her heart. She drifted in and out of sleep, restless, eager for morning to come.

She was dressed in her cabin, her letter to Daphne folded and sealed on the writing desk, when Father opened the door.

She tried not to flinch. He lowered dark eyebrows at her, his customary expression in the last few weeks as she had become more and more withdrawn from him.

"Constance," he said, "we have arrived in Table Bay. The crew are going ashore for two days. Do you have anything for the post?"

She offered up her letter, her heart sinking. "Father?" she ventured. "Could I . . . would it be possible for me to accompany you ashore?"

"I'm not going ashore. You're staying here, and somebody will have to watch you."

Ordinarily she might have protested how unfair this was, but she was utterly intimidated by him. "Very well," she said, and returned to her bed to gaze out the window at the mountain and the bay. Trying not to think how much she felt like one of Old Harry's doomed chickens in its coop.

———

Good Bess quit the Cape of Good Hope with a brisk gale after eight long days waiting for favorable winds. Henry was growing anxious, though he didn't know why. Sixteen years had passed since Faith's disappearance; the matter of a few days would hardly make a difference to the outcome of the journey. And yet anxious he was, keen to move, keen for the wind to blow.

Within a week, he was keen for it to stop blowing. Northwesterly gales plagued them. One particularly violent storm plunged him deep into fear. The swell was high, but kept down by the violence of the wind itself, which ripped the white tops off the waves and sent them hailing across the decks. He couldn't stay upright without holding the rail, and his roared commands were carried away from the ears they were meant for. "Hand the mainsail!"

he shouted, hoarse. "Take another reef in the mizzen topsail! For God's sake, keep *Bess* before the wind!"

He had been at sea nearly all his adult life, had steeled himself through storms twice the measure of this one. Why was he so fearful? Then it came to him: prior to this day, the only cargo he had carried was for trade. But today, Constance was aboard. His precious child. For all that she couldn't meet his eye, that she quavered when he approached as though he might eat her, he loved her and couldn't bear the thought of her coming to any harm.

———

They soon met with the south-east trade winds, blowing fresh and scented with the tropics. *Good Bess* was head-up for the Gulf of Mannar. Their journey was nearly complete.

———

"Captain?"

Henry turned from his navigation charts to see Maitland standing at the door to his cabin. He looked tense, and Henry felt himself tense up in sympathy. "Maitland?"

"We've seen a pearling schooner."

"We're sailing between pearl banks. Of course you've seen a pearling vessel."

Maitland cleared his throat. "We think it's de Locke's."

Henry's blood began to warm up. "You mean, you think it's *mine*."

Maitland nodded. Henry clasped his right fist in his left palm. "Prepare the men. We're going to take it. In one piece if we can. We'll fire three shots across her bow. If he still resists, we'll blow it to bits."

Maitland hurried off, and Henry took a moment to gather his thoughts. De Locke, that scoundrel. Four years ago, Henry had bought pearls from de Locke for a trader back in England. It was only through fortunate coincidence that one of his paying guests on *Good Bess* was a jeweller, who had looked at them and declared six of them to be made of painted clay. Henry pursued de Locke through the pearl fishery superintendent. De Locke immediately and conveniently forgot every word of English he knew, so Henry's journey home was delayed while a translator was sought.

Then, late in the evening, de Locke had come to see Henry aboard *Good Bess* and, in halting but perfectly comprehensible English, challenged him to a match of écarté, staking the money he owed on the outcome of the card game.

By lamplight in the low-ceilinged cabin, with Maitland and Burchfield as witnesses, they had played. Henry wasn't ordinarily a gambler, so de Locke had to provide the cards and refresh his memory to the game's rules. In two *voles*, de Locke had increased his debt to Henry threefold. He drank fiercely, bet recklessly, continued to increase his debt. Then, finally, he had pulled out the title deed to his pearler, *La Reine des Perles*, and thrown it on the table.

"All against this," he declared.

Henry agreed.

De Locke turned up three kings. Which was interesting since Henry also had two. Maitland searched de Locke's jacket and found high-scoring cards tucked into his sleeves. Under the threat of a pistol, de Locke was forced to count the cards, submit one correct deck, then roll his sleeves to his elbows for the final game. The one that everything was staked on.

De Locke was terrified now, perspiration beading above his gingery eyebrows. He turned over two tens, but Henry had two queens. And so he earned himself a third: the *Queen of Pearls*, as the pearler would be known in English.

Henry scooped up the title deed and crushed it in his fist.

"A pleasure doing business with you, Gilbert," he said.

De Locke looked as though he were fighting tears. "Will you give me until the morning to collect my things? Tell my crew?"

"Of course."

In hindsight, that had been foolish. De Locke disappeared within an hour. A visit to his home the next morning had discovered only empty rooms. Henry sailed, still in possession of the pearler's title deed, and without being repaid the money he was owed. He had always intended, some day, to track de Locke down and make him repay his debt. To happen across him in the Gulf of Mannar was luck too good to be ignored.

He left his cabin, intending to go up on deck. Then he saw Constance's cabin door and remembered himself.

"Constance?" he said, knocking briskly, then opening the door.

She sat at her writing desk, auburn hair unbound.

"Father?"

"No matter what happens in the next hour, no matter what you hear, you are to stay here in the cabin. Do you understand?"

She nodded, her eyes round with surprise . . . or was that fear? He hadn't time to debate it.

"Don't lean out the window, either. And put your trunk in front of the door. Just in case."

Who knew what de Locke was capable of?

Another nod. Why did she look so pale? What cause had he given her to be so afraid of him? "Don't worry, child," he said, unable to keep the impatience out of his voice. "I know what I'm doing."

He left, closing the door behind him. He could hear the sound of her shifting her trunk. Good, at least she'd listened to him. Heart thudding, he made his way up, hoping the gunners had the cannons ready.

———

"Tell them it's not good enough, Alexandre!" barked de Locke.

Alexandre turned to his diving companions, translated de Locke's words but softened them. "He wants to know if you can work faster. It's been a bad month." The pearl tucked in his cheek seemed to burn a guilty hole. No pearls in four weeks—only the one that Alexandre had found—and de Locke was growing frantic.

"We are working as fast as we can for the money he is paying us," one of the divers said in response.

Alexandre turned to de Locke, hedged, then said, "They say they will do their best."

"Don't mumble so," de Locke said, gruffly, turning away.

Alexandre adjusted the mainsail sheet, then glanced up. A ship had been growing closer all morning, but now she was clearly visible, the English merchant flag flying from her masthead. Alexandre watched a few moments. It seemed the ship was bearing straight for them, approaching fast.

"Gilbert?"

De Locke joined him, peering at the ship. "English pigs. What do they want?"

A sudden gust made the pearler heel over. Alexandre, perched on the cabin top watching the larger ship, lost his footing and crashed into the pin rail, cracking his jaw. He fell to the deck. The pain echoed through his skull. He shook his head hard, fighting unconsciousness.

De Locke was leaning over him, slapping his face. "Boy? Boy? Are you well?"

Alexandre opened his mouth wide to test his jaw. De Locke's eyes seized on something within. Alexandre snapped his mouth shut hard, but it was too late.

The pistol was at his temple a half-second later. "What are you hiding in there?"

Alexandre shook his head. De Locke cocked the gun.

"Answer me!" he screamed. "What are you hiding in there? Alexandre, how could you?"

Then the voice boomed to them on the wind, made brassy and flat by the speaking trumpet. "You can give her up now, or we will use force."

De Locke's head snapped around. "Blackchurch!" he spat.

Alexandre saw his chance and scrambled to his feet. A gunshot followed him. He ran to the side of the ship and dived.

———

Constance curled up on her bed, pulling the covers over her head. Father had looked so fearsome, his eyes glittering, anger and excitement threaded through every muscle of his body. She could hear shouted commands, the cannons being wheeled into place. Something awful was going to happen, she just knew it. Then she heard Father's voice through the speaking trumpet.

"You can give her up now, or we will use force."

Tears squeezed out from under closed eyelids. It was true then—Father was a pirate and he couldn't even control his impulses on this one journey with his daughter aboard. She wanted to run up there and stop him, tear the gunners' hands off the cannons, plead with her father for life and mercy. But the image of him in her dream returned, of the pistol levelled at her head.

Minutes passed; nothing happened. In the distance she could hear gunshots.

Then a huge thundering bang clattered through the ship. She pulled her pillow over her head and screamed into it, sobbing. Another bang. She tried to burrow further into her bed, but the mattress was hard, unyielding. Another bang.

She sat up and howled, terrified and overwhelmed. Men's voices shouting, sounds of water, splashing. She ignored Father's warning, put her face to the window. The captain of the other ship—a small pearler—and two native crewmen stood at the starboard of the vessel, hands raised in a gesture of surrender. One of *Good Bess*'s boats was on its way across the distance, Maitland at the helm, six crewmen with him. Why would Father bother to raid such a small vessel? It seemed cruel, and her heart ached for the captain, a doughy man with springy red curls, who looked frightened sick. What would they do to him now? She'd heard awful things about pirates: plank-walking, throat-cutting, keel-hauling. Her heart fluttered, and she felt she might faint. As the boat pulled up alongside the pearler, she had to look away.

As she did so, a head popped out of the water on the other side of *Good Bess.* Startled, she fell back onto her bed. She had to climb up and look again. A man, perhaps a few years older than herself. He must have come off the pearler, swum underwater . . . how was that possible without his being seen? He was looking up at the ship, looking up, she realized, at her. With pleading eyes.

Constance glanced from the young man to the scene over at the pearler, then back again. And determination gripped her. She wouldn't let Father do his horrible deeds to all those innocent men. She could save at least one of them.

"Wait," she called. She went to her door, kicked the trunk aside, and hurried out, past cabins to the main-deck steerage, where she found a long rope. She took it back to her cabin, careful to close her door behind her and seal it with the trunk again—against pirates—and tied the rope around the foot of her bed. Being a seaman's daughter had its benefits; she had been able to tie a thousand different knots since her eighth birthday.

She cast the other end of the rope down to the young man, who climbed up through her window and landed, sopping wet, on her bed.

"Are you well, sir?" she asked. "You were underwater for a long time."

He stood, looking at her, but didn't speak. She realized he might not know English. She also realized that he had the darkest eyes she had ever seen, almost black, miles deep. Time slowed as she measured the depth of those eyes; a slow flush suffused her skin, from her toes to her scalp.

She shook her head. Why was she thinking such things at a time like this? "I have no dry clothes for you," she said.

He shrugged, to show he didn't mind being wet. So he did understand her. Why, then, didn't he speak?

"I'm Constance. I'm the captain's daughter. I'm sorry—I didn't know he was . . . I'm so sorry." The tears squeezed out again, and the young man stood in a growing pool of seawater, looking at her with his bottomless eyes and saying nothing.

"I don't . . . I don't know what to do now. He'll come. We'll have to hide you. Get you ashore somehow. We're going to Ceylon. I'll keep you safe. I'll . . ." She met his gaze, tried a smile. "What is your name? Can you tell me?"

The corners of his mouth lifted in a smile—and seemed to lift the corners of her heart with it. He barely opened his lips, but his name came out clearly nonetheless.

"Alexandre," he said. "And I am in your debt."

Chapter 7

GULF OF MANNAR

Constance opened her mouth to ask another question, one that she forgot instantly when the brisk knocking at the door commenced.

"Constance? It's your father. You can open the door now."

Constance yelped, pushed Alexandre into the corner behind the dresser. "Hide," she hissed.

"I need to speak to the captain," he muttered.

"No, you must hide. He's dangerous."

"I must ask him for a passage. I can pay him."

"But he's—"

The knock became thunderous, Father's voice alarmed. "Constance? Are you there? What's wrong? Are you harmed?" He began to push against the door; the trunk began to move.

"I'm fine!" she called shrilly. "Don't come in, I'm . . ."

She couldn't think quickly enough. "I'm dressing," she said.

"You're already dressed. I saw you this morning. What's going on?" Then he stopped talking and started shoving, and the trunk slipped in short jumps across the floorboards. She pushed Alexandre's head down, and he crouched behind the dresser while she ran to the door.

With her foot, she pushed the trunk out of the way. The door fell open. Father glared at her. "What's wrong? You're shaking."

"All the noise. It frightened me." Her mind was scrambling for lies, but not quickly enough. Father's eyes caught on something behind her. She turned. Alexandre was standing up, in clear sight. What on earth was he thinking?

Father pulled out his pistol, thumbed back the striker and aimed it at Alexandre. It was too similar to her nightmare. Reality grew sharp edges. Her heart seemed to catch on her ribs. "No! Don't kill him! Don't kill him, you scoundrel!" she shouted, kicking her father in the shin.

Father turned to her, an expression of anger and shock in his eyes. Alexandre put his hand to his lips, then held it out. On his palm was a gleaming pearl.

"Captain, I am Alexandre Sans-Nom, and I require only a passage home to France," he said, clearly now. "This is everything I have."

"What the blazes are you doing in my daughter's cabin?"

Constance rushed in. "It's my fault, Father! I let him in. I thought you were going to kill him."

Father shook his head incredulously, returning the pistol's striker to the safe position and tucking it at his waistband. "I might have killed him, Constance. But only because he's in your cabin. How did he get on board?"

Constance indicated the rope tied to the leg of her bed.

"Are you mad? You know nothing about him. He might be a scurvy knave. He might have—"

All her feelings welled up into her throat, demanding to be released. "He's an innocent man! Like the other men on that ship you just took by force. I know you're a pirate, but are you a murderer too?"

"Please, sir," Alexandre continued, calmly. Constance could hear he had a French accent. "I am done with de Locke. I want only to return to my homeland. Don't send me back to him."

"Back to France? We're at war with France!" Father

looked from one of them to the other, his palms up as though he didn't know whether to slap their faces or block his ears. "Listen to the both of you. Not an ounce of sense between you. Young man, keep your jewelry. You will be incarcerated in the hold until I can decide what to do with you. Don't worry, I won't send you back to de Locke because I know too well what kind of a man he is. And Constance, I need to speak with you, for you have formed an opinion of me that . . ." He trailed off into red-faced frustration. "I need to speak with you," he repeated quietly. "Wait here."

He took Alexandre by the elbow.

"Don't hurt him!" she called.

"Of course I won't hurt him," he replied hotly.

Alexandre went with Father willingly, falling once again to silence. Constance sat on her bed, heart thundering and face hot. Should she try to escape? Surely Father wouldn't harm her, would he?

Hours later, he came back. She had spent the intervening time calming herself, reminding herself that a man who loaned his daughter his only pillow would not also want to shoot her. But in the process, she made herself sad. She had lost her mother, and her father terrified her. All she had was Violet and Daphne, and they were so far away. She felt mournful, homesick, sorry for herself. Waiting and waiting for Father's return.

"Come on, lass," he said, taking her by the elbow. "We'll go up to the poop. I think we both need a good dose of fresh air."

She allowed herself to be led. Outside, the sky had silvered to twilight, pale pink clouds lay over the rolling waves. Constance was surprised to see that they were near land. The ship was hove-to, sails arranged so it would bob quietly in the water, so she knew they would not be staying here for long. Sea birds circled overhead. As she climbed the ladder to the poop, she saw that the ship's boat was arrowing away towards a small, overgrown island. Maitland rowed the boat, and the captain of the pearler, de Locke, sat guarded by two other crewmen.

"What are you going to do with him?" Constance asked, pausing on the ladder.

Father, who was already above, gave an irritated grunt. "Come, child. Don't dither."

She climbed up and joined him on the poop. He was leaning on the rail, watching the boat's journey. She waited, her mouth dry. He turned, eyebrows momentarily angry. With visible effort, he tried to smile. "Constance, I am not what you think I am."

She didn't know how to answer, so she said nothing.

"De Locke is an old enemy. The *Queen of Pearls* is mine, won in a dispute over money. I own the title deed. He stole her."

Now she was puzzled.

"As to your question about what we will do with him, we are going to leave him on that island with provisions enough to sustain him until we are well away. This is a common trade route; somebody will find him before long. But he is not trustworthy, and I don't want him following us."

Constance looked around. "Where's the pearler?"

"Two of my men have already sailed her off to Nagakodi. We'll meet with them in a day or so, good winds permitting. I'll sell her and recover my money. De Locke's crew are all in the hold. I intend to take the two natives to the pearl fisheries superintendent at Puttalam before we head to Nagakodi. They are both originally from Ceylon and will be well taken care of there."

"And Alexandre?" She remembered those dark eyes, his calmness in the face of her fearsome father, the heat that had tingled in her toes being so close to his damp body.

"I am still deciding what to do with Alexandre." He glanced away. "But I won't harm him, if that was your next question." Constance bit her lip. It was.

Once again he met her eye, then, to her very great surprise, took her hand. "I am sorry if you are afraid of me, child. I have given you no just cause, and so I can only assume that you have somehow ignored my rules and mingled with the crew, overhearing some fragment of untruth that has grown nightmarish in your brain."

She swallowed hard. Nodded. She could see the effort it took him not to berate her.

"What did you hear?" he asked, in a forcedly even tone.

"That you were a pirate," she whispered. "A long time ago."

He sighed. "I was never a pirate. I am a merchant seaman and have always been so. But . . ."

Constance waited, breath suspended.

"Shortly after your mother disappeared . . . I was not myself. My first run after the . . . event was to the Malabar Coast, to Cochin. I had a special charge from a very rich man, a cargo to pick up. Sixty crates of tea. He was willing to pay much higher than the East India Company, so I took the commission. But we had weeks of bad weather. Gales, squalls, then we were becalmed in the doldrums, on the equator, for sixteen days. I arrived at Cochin a month later than expected. Exhausted, still frantic about Faith, wondering if she had returned in my absence . . ." He paused, and Constance found that she was blinking back tears. "I was not in the mood for what happened.

"A wily Portuguese captain had heard about the commission, about my failure to pick it up yet. He persuaded the local seller to let him take it. So my rich cargo was gone. The trip had been all for nothing. I gathered together an alternate cargo, small, low-paying items. Letters home to England by the sackful. And we made our way back. Then, near the Mascarene Islands, one of my crew spotted a Portuguese ship."

Father stopped and gazed off into the distance. He was silent a long time.

Finally, Constance said, "Was it the ship that had taken your cargo?"

Father shook his head, smiling ruefully. "No. Of course not. That ship was weeks ahead of us. This was simply a ship flying the Portuguese flag. I knew that, the crew knew that, and yet . . . and yet we wanted somebody to be punished for what had happened and there it was. . . ."

He put his hand to his head, rubbing his eyebrow with the heel of his palm. "There it was."

He straightened, smoothed his waistcoat and nodded decisively. "It was regrettable. No man was injured— they were a much smaller vessel and surrendered quickly. We incarcerated the crew. I sent a man aboard to sail it alongside us to the nearest port. By this time, I realized my folly and set them all free, letting them keep their cargo. On my return to England I made a full confession to the Company and was ordered to pay reparation. They were lenient with me on account of my good record thus far and on account of the recent loss of my wife. I spent a month in prison, Constance, when you were little more than a babe." He hung his head, and Constance realized he was ashamed. "You wouldn't have noticed; you were used to my being away."

"Father, I'm so sorry."

There was a long quiet, when all she could hear was the sound of the waves splashing against the ribs of the ship. So the Irishman had not told the truth, but an exaggerated rumor. She felt foolish, ashamed. When Father spoke again, it was so softly that she barely heard him. "If your mother had died, Constance, it would have been easier."

It was true. Not knowing was the worst of it. "What

do you think happened to her?" she asked, dreading the answer. In the distance, the boat had started its journey back to *Good Bess*. De Locke was gone.

"I don't know. But she was a strong woman. I know she could survive much hardship."

"Then why did she not come back?"

"Perhaps she has no recollection of us. Or perhaps she is constrained somehow. We know she has been here, across the miles. If she has no money, no way to get home . . ." He shook his head. "There is no benefit in speculation. I will uncover all the clues I can and, God willing, bring her home with me."

"I want to help, too," Constance said. "Will you let me help you, Father? I have a good brain. I don't want to be stuck at home with Howlett's daughter. I don't—"

"How do you know about Howlett's daughter?"

A rush of heat. Constance's heart began to pound. "I . . . you must have told me."

"Indeed no, I did not tell you."

She forced a laugh. "Well, you must have, Father because I . . . I know of her."

"I deliberately made no mention of Orlanda because I was not certain that she would be at home and did not want to raise your expectations of a companion." He folded his arms across his chest. "Constance, did you read my letter to Violet?"

She finally knew the true meaning of the word "speechless." She literally could not speak.

His temper, held in check for the entire conversation, finally escaped him. "I have clearly misjudged you. Here I am, treating you like an adult, when you are little more than a willful child." He began to stride away from her.

"Father, wait!"

"No, Constance. No. I have business to take care of. I have spent enough time on you. We will be in Nagakodi within thirty-six hours. I will speak to you again then."

And he was gone.

Constance left her cabin that evening, intending to go up on deck for her usual dose of fresh night air. But she stopped, uncomfortable at the thought of seeing Father again. And so minutes passed; paused in indecision outside her cabin, her thoughts turned to Alexandre. She wondered if Old Harry had brought him and his companions supper, whether he was comfortable, whether Father had decided to take him back to France. She couldn't ask Father all these things, and Old Harry had maintained his silence with her.

Would it be such a bad thing to ask Alexandre himself? The thought gave her a warm thrill, deep inside. Just that morning, he had stood—dripping wet—in her cabin. So close. Since then, she hadn't seen him, and he had become almost like a storybook figure. Not real.

She wavered. She was already in so much trouble with Father. . . . But then, he couldn't be any angrier with her than he was now.

Constance made her way down to the lower-deck hold. By the dim light, she saw him. His shoulder was turned to her, his knees to his chest, arms wrapped around them. The two Sinhalese men were talking softly to each other. Father had the three of them in the cattle pen, on fresh straw, cuffs of steel around their ankles. She felt a pang of embarrassment. Why must he chain them? They weren't criminals. The smell of the hold was awful, and there was so little air that the candle could barely burn.

Alexandre must have heard her and turned to look over his shoulder. When he saw her, he stood.

"Hello," she said softly.

The corner of his mouth lifted, a subdued smile. "Good evening, Miss Blackchurch."

The formality stung. "You may call me Constance." She moved forward, so she could see him properly. Tall and dark-eyed, with tanned skin, his black hair hanging loose to his shoulders. Yes, he was real. More than real, for he focused all her senses sharply, making the surroundings fade and blur.

"Very well, Constance."

She noticed a large bruise across his jaw. She leaned closer to peer at it. "What's that? Has somebody hit you? My father?"

"No, no. It's an old injury." He lowered his head. "I am in your father's debt. He has treated us well."

She wasn't expecting this answer. "Really?"

One of the Sinhalese men, a lean man with big hands, looked up and said something to Alexandre in his native tongue.

Alexandre nodded, then returned his attention to Constance. "He says your father is a good man."

"You speak Sinhalese?"

"De Locke and I lived in Ceylon for some years."

She indicated the cuffs. "I'm so sorry about the chains."

"I spoke to your father at length this afternoon. He said he'd send somebody to release us this evening. He didn't have the key."

Her heart jumped. She didn't want to be discovered

down here with Alexandre. But at the same time, she was finding it very difficult to pull away from him.

"Has he decided what to do with you, then?"

"I told him that *La Reine des Perles* has been my home for many years. When we anchor, he will let me stay aboard, take care of her, until he finds a buyer in Ceylon. Then I am to return to England with *Good Bess*. He won't take payment—he says I can work for my passage. I can sell my pearl in England and have enough to get home to France and to start a new life. An independent one." Here he smiled fully, and she felt her heart flip over.

"Oh, that's . . . wonderful." Weeks and weeks. She would have weeks and weeks with him around. Then she put the thought out of her head. It wasn't as though Father would let her see him.

"Constance, I must thank you for your assistance, for helping me aboard."

She gestured to his companions. "You would have ended up here anyway."

A shadow crossed his brow. "Maybe. But I didn't know that at the time, and you were generous enough to reach out to a stranger."

She moved a little closer, put her hands around the

bars of the pen. "How did you manage to swim away from the pearler without being seen?"

"It's my job to stay underwater for long stretches," he said, almost dismissively. Once again, Constance had the feeling that he wasn't telling the whole story. "Constance, I wonder if I might prevail upon your generosity once more?"

"Of course," she said too quickly.

He fished the pearl from the cuff of his pants and held it out to her. "Will you keep this safe? Perhaps you have a jewellery box? I can get it from you at the other end of our journey. In England."

She took the pearl, brushing his warm fingers with her own momentarily. "I will be most pleased to honor your trust." Then she heard voices and stepped away from the cattle pen in alarm. "I have to go," she said quickly.

"Thank you," he said again, his dark eyes evenly fixed on hers. "Most sincerely."

She felt herself blush, then blushed all the more, and was grateful for the dim light. "You're welcome. Most sincerely. Most, most sincerely." She backed away, stumbling over her feet. "I'll see you ashore? Perhaps?"

"I will follow your father's instructions."

Then she made her way aft, back through the ship

and up to the roundhouse, a tangle of hot feelings in her heart.

—•••—

De Locke slowly worked his way out of his ropes. They had tied him firmly but not tightly, giving themselves just enough time to get away. What did they think he would do if his hands were free before they were out of sight? They had taken his pistol, his ship, and his crew. All he had was the clothes on his back and a wretched basket with salted fish and half a loaf of bread in it. Did they think he would throw food at them?

Evening deepened to nighttime. The air was chill, but not cold. Still, he longed for his warm bed. How far was he from Tumkottai? He supposed he would hail a passing ship, or make his way by foot across the sand at low tide to the mainland—though all he could see from here was jungle and beaches. Anger began to burn bright inside him. Blackchurch. How had he found him? After all these years, de Locke had been sure he'd escaped his revenge. In all the wide oceans, across the Gulf of Mannar, how was it possible for Blackchurch to find *La Reine des Perles*?

And as for Alexandre . . . Week after week there had been no pearls, and here the boy had been hiding one all along. De Locke stamped his feet with frustration.

Alexandre had been quiet, mumbling if he spoke, and de Locke never once suspected it was because he was hiding a treasure in his mouth. Thief. Traitor.

Traitor. Suddenly, it was clear to de Locke. He had seen the girl help Alexandre aboard *Good Bess*, without a blink. Alexandre knew them. Somehow he had contacted Blackchurch, given him their whereabouts, invited him to take the pearler. . . . He wanted to weep, and because he wanted to weep—big, fat, helpless tears—he grew angrier and angrier until he roared across the island, "Alexandre!"

And he vowed not to return to Tumkottai at all. He vowed instead to track down his enemies, and make them pay in blood.

Chapter 8

NAGAKODI, NORTH-WESTERN CEYLON

Early-morning light suffused the sky, and the chatter of sea birds drifted to Alexandre's ears over the bay. He leaned on the starboard rail of *La Reine des Perles*, now anchored in Nagakodi's quiet harbor, and watched the boat row away from *Good Bess*.

They had cast anchor late at night, and Alexandre had been freed from the hull—his two companions had already been delivered into the hands of the fisheries superintendent—and taken directly across to the pearler, where he slept soundly in his usual hammock. With the first light, he'd heard the commotion on the ship as people and their luggage were readied to be taken ashore, and had come out to see if he could glimpse her, the captain's daughter. Constance.

What good it would do him to see her, he didn't know. Captain Blackchurch was not likely to let them form an attachment. Alexandre knew he was very low in the world. But he thought he had seen in her some spark, some particular kindness that ignored their social differences. And he found his thoughts returning to her. He thought himself a calm person, accepting, able to manage no matter what the circumstances. But being near Constance made him feel a tightness he was unaccustomed to—as though his muscles were coiled in readiness for something, as though bright energy hummed within him.

There she was. Her fair face was hidden under a wide-brimmed bonnet. Her auburn hair caught the white morning sun, her back was very erect. She turned to look over her shoulder, saw him and lifted her hand in a tentative wave. He returned the wave, equally tentative. Blackchurch was scowling, but Alexandre wasn't certain whether it was directed at him or just a sign of more general crankiness. He lowered his hand, leaned his forearms on the railing and breathed the light morning air.

Blackchurch wanted the pearler readied for sale. Alexandre had maintained it well over the years, but de Locke had skimped on some repairs. Many of the seams needed caulking, and her topsides needed a fresh coat of paint.

He hoped, though, that it wouldn't take long. He hadn't much of an idea when Blackchurch intended to return to England; Alexandre would have to ask him directly. The thought of being here too long made Alexandre nervous, because he knew de Locke. He wouldn't let his livelihood go so easily.

Alexandre tried to put such anxious thoughts from his mind. The boat had skidded up onto sand. Bending palm trees caught the sun on their leaves as Constance gracefully climbed out of the boat, looking around her. He wondered what she was thinking. Was she admiring the raw beauty of the place? Or, like so many of the travellers here, comparing it unfavorably with the compact dampness of England?

He smiled. He liked to imagine that she saw the beauty, that she could think outside the well-worn tracks of her countrymen, find something to like about this unsophisticated place. Because that just might mean she could find something to like about him.

Constance gazed up at the doric columns of William Howlett's villa. They dazzled white like marble, but marble was not found easily in these parts. Rather, it was a mix of lime and crushed oyster shells spread over the stone. Constance gazed at the double chimneys, the stone parapet and the portico. There was no concession at all to the local style of architecture. It was a little piece of England, here in Ceylon.

The villa was half a mile from the beach. Most of the crew were staying on board the ship, except for Mr. Burchfield and the two officers who were staying with a Dutch family in town. Constance could still hear the ocean, but it no longer moved underneath her. So accustomed to the swell was she that her body seemed to remember the motion in all her muscles. It was a strange feeling, like a soft twitching.

Father led her up to the front door of the villa, and knocked purposely. Maitland had been to see Howlett late last night, when they first cast anchor, and had arranged the visit formally.

The door opened. A beautiful native woman, with her black hair pinned up under a cloth cap, opened the door, smiled and said in perfect English, "Good morning, I am Chandrika. Won't you come in? I will fetch Mr. and Mrs. Howlett."

She left them in a large, quiet reception hall, with a patterned wooden floor. A housemaid was dusting a bust of Cicero, and the dust rose and spun slowly in the sunlit air. A squeal of delight from the top of the wide staircase broke the peace. "Company!"

Constance looked up to see a pretty girl of about her own age, with pale-blonde hair and a pointed nose, hurrying down the staircase with extreme excitement. She approached Constance with alarming speed, grabbing her with such force that she dropped her trunk and nearly overbalanced.

"Oh, a friend!" the girl said. "You've no idea how bored I've been!" She stood back to smile at Constance, who smiled warily in return. "I'm Orlanda," she said.

"Constance," Constance replied.

"I just know we will be the best of friends."

Father gave them a satisfied smile, clearly thinking that Constance had now found a companion as silly as the one she had left at home, and that he would no longer be bothered by her.

"Orlanda, show some decorum please!" This stern voice came from William Howlett, who had slipped into the room unnoticed. He smiled apologetically at Father. "Being in these parts works on the minds of the young. The wildness seeps in. I can barely constrain her to wear stockings and shoes some days." He rubbed papery hands together. "Please, come through to the sitting room. My wife is indisposed; she's only comfortable on her sofa. Leave your bags here, the maids will take care of them."

Howlett was a whip-thin man, taller than Father by a head. He was unusually pale, his neck hunched at an odd angle. He wore a fine, embroidered frock-coat and a silk cravat at his neck, and his thinning grey-streaked hair was neatly secured at the nape of his neck. Howlett had been an agent to the East India Company and made his fortune with them. Now he owned a small company, specializing in spices and jewels.

Orlanda squeezed Constance's hand all the way to the sitting room, which was a large, light-filled room facing east into a deep spice garden. The shutters were open, and the smell of cinnamon, ginger, and cloves was strong and sweet. Mrs. Howlett was semi-reclined on a sofa that had intricately carved legs. She had a quilted blanket pulled up as far as her lap, where her white hands lay limp.

She smiled weakly as her guests entered the room. "Good day, good day. I am very sorry, I am not feeling well."

Orlanda leaned close to Constance's ear and said, "She's never feeling well." Then she giggled.

Howlett glared at them both. "None of your silliness, young ladies."

Constance wanted to protest that *she* hadn't whispered, *she* hadn't giggled, and she most certainly was not silly. But greetings and polite conversations were now taking place all around her, tea was being fetched, and Orlanda was rolling her eyes and drawing Constance to stand with her by the cold fireplace.

"There's not much to do about here," Orlanda said. "It was much better at Colombo. I had friends; there were parties. . . ." She trailed off wistfully.

Constance, aware she had hardly spoken yet, asked, "Why did you leave Colombo?"

"Oh, Father started this new business a year ago. He wanted to be nearer the pearl fisheries." She dropped her gaze momentarily. "Besides, he wanted me away from Colombo."

"Why?"

She glanced up to see if her parents were listening. They weren't, both too engrossed in their conversations with Father. "There was a boy," she said. "Thomas. A nice English boy." She giggled. "You know?"

Constance didn't know, but she nodded anyway.

"Oh, it all got a little mad. Lord knows I didn't encourage him. Well, not *that* much. He was discovered trying to climb into my window one night. What a to-do!" Her blue eyes went heavenwards, sparkling with mischief. "Oh, I laughed and laughed. Father didn't see the humor in it. So, how long will you be staying?"

"I don't know," Constance replied, thinking, *Not long, I hope.* "Father has some business to take care of . . ."

"I do hope it's for months and months, as I have been so lonely and so bored." She turned to her parents. "Father, Mother? May I show Constance to our room?"

Howlett bustled over. "Constance is not sharing a room with you, Orlanda."

"But I specifically asked—"

"We have enough space here for Miss Blackchurch to have her own room. If I put you two in together, you'd never get a wink of sleep, up all night giggling and telling secrets."

Again, Constance was stung by the assumption that she was so foolish.

"But you can't put her on the western side!" Orlanda protested. "The noisy sea will bother her. It never stops, you know."

"She can close her window if she is so bothered."

"At least let me take her up to show her."

"Very well."

Orlanda seized Constance's hand and dragged her

through to the entrance hall and up the stairs, chattering all the time. "How rude it is to put you on the sea side of the house," she said.

"I like the sound of the sea."

"Nonsense, you needn't be polite about it. It would have been much better for you to share my room. Perhaps in a few days, when everything has settled again, you might ask Father specially. One can't hear the sea from my room, and when one wakes in the morning one can almost imagine one is back in England and not on a horrid salty island in the middle of nowhere." Orlanda drew breath. She opened the heavy wooden door to a cool, dim room. "When the sun reaches this side of the house, the heat is unbearable for a few hours. We normally take cool tea on the eastern veranda at that time of day."

Constance opened the mullioned windows, letting in the fresh sea air. She could see the wide bay, boats coming and going, *Good Bess* dominating the scene. Her eyes worked hard to find Alexandre's pearler. There it was. She wondered what he was doing now and remembered his pearl, which she had safely locked away in her trunk. "I could watch the sun set from here," she said.

"If you had a mind to."

She turned to Orlanda, untying her bonnet. "Do you not have a mind to watch sunsets?"

"What's the point? There will be another tomorrow."

A soft footfall near the door caught their attention. Mrs. Howlett stood there, supported by Chandrika.

"I will return to my bed," Mrs. Howlett said. "I hope you don't think me rude, Constance."

Constance could see the woman was trembling. "Of course not, Mrs. Howlett. If you're not well, you should be a-bed."

They shuffled off down the hall. Orlanda flopped onto Constance's bed, while Constance hung her bonnet on the corner of the dressing-table mirror. "I'm sorry your mother isn't well," she said.

"She's never well."

"What is it that ails her?"

"Nothing."

Constance sat with Orlanda, puzzled. "It must be something."

"Nothing that is an illness."

"I don't know what you mean."

"I'm sure Mother would be well enough if she stopped drinking laudanum."

Laudanum, Constance knew, was a mixture of opium

and alcohol. She had heard of people who grew addicted to the medicine, who suffered horrors and daytime nightmares from its overuse.

"Medicinally, of course," Orlanda added, though her ironic tone showed she didn't believe it. "I don't mind so much, Constance. With Mother always indisposed, and Father so busy with his work, nobody has much interest in what I do, or where I go." She sat up suddenly. "Come, let me show you the rest of the villa."

Room by room, Constance was introduced to the place that would be her home for the next short while. She liked the look of the library, on the lower floor, with French doors leading to an overgrown garden. Hibiscus grew in profusion, brightly colored blooms catching the morning light on their petals. On the other side was a long colonnade of wood, with a roof over it made of layers of coconut palm leaves. Lamps were suspended from the beams; tidy flagstones made up the floor. The untamed garden encroached on three sides, and the beach ran off from the third. To the north, Constance's eyes were drawn up the hill to a gleaming pagoda.

"This is a dancing room," Orlanda said with a sigh. "If it can be said to be a room when there are no walls. If it can be said that it's for dancing when I am the only soul who has a mind to dance." Orlanda's eyes lit up, a sudden realization seizing her. "Do you like to dance, Constance?"

"Of course."

"Only, I wonder if I can convince Father to arrange a party. There are some Dutch girls in town, sailors *everywhere* . . . we could send out the invitation all the way to Puttalam. Imagine . . ." She spread her arms out. "We could decorate this area with ribbons. Father could pay for musicians to come up from Colombo, or down from Kandy. Oh, Constance, is it not a wonderful idea?"

Constance agreed, but reluctantly so. After all, if she was consumed with organizing a dance, she wouldn't have much time to search for her mother. And even less to sit quietly on her own and think about Alexandre.

"It's settled then. I shall ask Father, and he shall say yes, of course; and this afternoon we will go into the town to order paper for invitations. Do you have a fair hand? I confess I write too hastily and spoil all my letters."

"Yes, I have a fair hand," Constance said.

"I should have guessed, for you are very calm and probably quite sensible. Father always says I haven't an ounce of brain between my ears, and I suppose him to be right." Orlanda sighed and squeezed Constance's hand again. And Constance felt her resistance to her new friend melt away. Yes, she was spirited, silly, overbearing. But any girl who had been told she was stupid by her father would probably have turned out that way. She felt reluctantly glad for her own father momentarily, that he had bothered to insist on a good education for her.

"Come, let us practice our steps, as it has been an age since I danced," Orlanda said, pulling Constance into the middle of the dance floor. "I shall be most shame-faced if I can't manage a simple quadrille."

Once the girls were gone, once Mrs. Howlett had retired, trembling, to her room, Henry was alone with Howlett at last. He waited only a few polite seconds before pouncing on him with questions. "What news? Any?"

"I've not heard another thing since that first day," Howlett said. "That a woman named Blackchurch had spent considerable time here, in Nagakodi, some twelve years past. I confess, I haven't much asked about it though, as my business keeps me well occupied."

Henry was chastened. "Of course. Of course. I shouldn't expect you to help me. It's my problem, so—"

"Of course I will help you, old friend," Howlett said, hands spread expansively. "I am quite an expert in the local language and will happily translate for you."

"And in return, I will help you with your business. If there is anything I can do. Adding up accounts, writing letters . . ."

"Very well, it sounds like a fair exchange of time and skills. I am always terribly busy." Howlett went to the fireplace and leaned on the mantelpiece. "I expect the place to start is in the town, back at the markets where I first heard mention." Howlett offered him a strained smile, then spoke hesitantly. "Henry, have you really thought this through? You know that you might . . . discover things that are hard to know."

"But at least I will know," Henry said gruffly, uncomfortable talking about his feelings.

Howlett, clearly just as uncomfortable, backed away from the question happily. "Very well, then. Rest a little while to recover from your journey, and after dinner we will start our campaign."

Constance and Orlanda were dressed in their town clothes, fastening their bonnets against the brilliant sunshine, when they ran into Alexandre on the front path up to the villa.

"Oh," Orlanda said, speechless for the first time that day.

Constance's heart swelled again, and she couldn't stop herself smiling. "Hello, Alexandre," she said shyly.

"Good day." He had tied back his hair, but his feet were still bare.

Remembering her manners, she gestured towards Orlanda. "This is Miss Howlett."

"Orlanda," she said, finding her voice.

"This is Alexandre," Constance said, tasting his name on her tongue again. "He is repairing a ship for Father." She hoped that didn't sound like she thought he was a servant.

"You're a carpenter, then?" Orlanda asked.

"I'm actually a pearl diver. At least, that's what I've done the last seven years."

Orlanda smiled coyly. "Do I detect a French accent?" Then, without waiting for an answer, she launched into a stream of very bad French. "I am pleased very to make our much acquaintance, and hope that you do too."

Alexandre was clearly battling with an urge to laugh, and Constance reminded herself never to speak a word of her own clunky French—why, oh why had she not listened to Mademoiselle Girard?—lest she too arouse his amusement. Alexandre answered in French, "The pleasure is all mine, Orlanda."

Orlanda blushed, and Constance experienced an uncomfortable bolt of jealousy. Orlanda was so pretty, pale-eyed and girlish. Constance was too tall, too dark.

"Well, I must say, your English is better than my French," Orlanda said.

"He speaks Sinhalese as well," Constance put in, keen to demonstrate how well she already knew him.

"Ah, now that is a boon. My father thinks he speaks Sinhalese, but in fact he has the poorest grasp of the language. Why, he was showing off to visitors one time and asked Chandrika for a fork to stir his tea rather than a spoon. Chandrika, who has quite a sense of humor, brought it without correcting him. He took the fork without a blink and pretended it was a local custom." Orlanda giggled. "Oh, I have stood too long in the sun and feel quite light-headed. Shall we return to the shade of the veranda? I'll send Chandrika to make us tea."

Alexandre became flustered as he realized the invitation was extended to him. "I . . . really only came to see the captain."

"Father's not home," Constance said. "He and Mr. Howlett have gone to town." She didn't remind Orlanda that they were to meet their fathers in town in two hours. She had become very invested in the idea of taking tea with Alexandre, especially without Father around.

"And Mother is unwell in her room, so you see it is all settled. I am the mistress of the house, and I declare we shall have tea on the veranda. Come." Orlanda led them back up the path and insisted they all sit around the wide teak table, shaded under a frangipani tree overgrown with vines. Chandrika proved difficult to find, and so Orlanda reluctantly left Constance and Alexandre alone for a few minutes while she made the tea.

"Why did you need to see Father?" she asked him, when the uncomfortable silence had drawn out too long. "Is there anything I can help with?"

"I need to ask him about paint," he said dismissively. Then, a moment later, "But perhaps you can help. Do you know how long your father intends to stay here?"

"His business here is . . . uncertain," she said guardedly. "There's no way of knowing."

Alexandre was clearly puzzled, but too polite to ask further questions. She was seized by the horrible fear that he would think she withheld the truth from him because of the difference in their social situations.

"It's personal," she blurted. "It's . . ." Then she stopped herself, wondered why she was keeping the story about her mother secret from Alexandre at all. He could speak the local language; he might be able to help. She glanced about, checking that Orlanda was not on her way back yet.

"Alexandre," she said, "can I trust you in confidence?"

"Of course," he said, his intense eyes fixed on her. "Only, don't tell me anything that you will later regret."

Opening her mouth, sharing her secret, felt delicious, a secret thrill. She realized, dimly, that she was tying herself to him in a small way. The whole story came out: her mother's disappearance, Howlett hearing of her, Constance stowing away on *Good Bess*. But before she could get to her point, that she hoped he might help her in her search, Orlanda returned with a tea tray.

"Well, I don't know where Chandrika is. But here, I've made us a tolerable afternoon tea, nonetheless." She smiled brightly as she sat. "So, what have you two been talking about?"

"The weather," Constance said.

"Not much weather here, is there? Just hot and sunny, or hot and rainy." She began to pour the tea, serving it with brown sugar and lemon. For all that she was terrible at French, and a self-confessed ninny, Orlanda made wonderful tea.

Alexandre cleared his throat. "I would like to say,

ladies," he said hesitantly, "that I am at your disposal, both of you, should you think of any way I can help you." He nodded particularly towards Constance, and she hid her smile behind her tea cup, knowing that the offer was intended directly for her.

She didn't know what was more exciting: that she had somebody to help in her quest to find her mother, or that the somebody was Alexandre.

Chapter 9

As Henry walked into town with Howlett, all he could think was, *Faith was here.* Howlett talked the whole way, and Henry hmmed in the right places, but really his mind was focused on the thought that his wife had once been here. Along the narrow dirt road, past the gleaming pagoda, alongside the houses—mudbrick and coconut palm leaves or tidy stone villas built by the Dutch—and then into the chattering market, its intoxicating mixture of smells permeating the balmy air . . . he wondered how Faith had experienced it, how she had felt, what she had thought of when her feet trod this very road. If she had thought of him.

"This is the one," Howlett said, pulling up short at a market stall with an aging, but sharp-eyed, Sinhalese woman behind it. She climbed to her feet with difficulty, barely raising a smile for them.

Howlett began to speak to her in Sinhalese. Henry wished he understood what was going on. The woman appeared to grow impatient, repeating herself, while Howlett slipped in and out of English. Finally, he nodded and she sat back down.

"What? What is it?" Henry asked.

"It's the same thing I overheard last time. The Blackchurch woman—they've translated the words into their own tongue, black church—lived some years ago in a little place to the north of the main square." He indicated with his hand. The woman began to speak again, saying the same word over and over. Howlett looked at her puzzled, then said, "Ah." He changed arms. "To the *south* of the main square."

"A house? Which house? Does she know which one?"

"She's given me quite clear instructions," Howlett said. "We can go there now."

Henry's heart puffed up with hope. "Now? Wonderful! How do you say thank you? I want to thank her."

"*Irida*," Howlett said, checking his pocket watch on its chain.

"*Irida*," Henry said to the woman.

She gave him an amused raise of the eyebrows. "*Istuti*," she said.

Henry turned to Howlett, who said, "Oh. Yes. Quite right. *Istuti* is thank you. *Irida* means Sunday. Come along."

Henry followed Howlett, wondering how much confidence he should have in his friend's language skills.

The sun grew hot above them, and Henry tried to stick to the shade as they wove out of town on the muddy road and back down the hill into a densely vegetated valley. The last street belonging to the town beckoned on their right, and Howlett led Henry down it with confidence. Here and there, elephant tracks had created holes in the mud. They had filled with scummed water; bugs zipped around them eagerly. The houses were a mishmash of colonial and native features, mostly ill-kept. Howlett stopped in front of the second-last one on the street, gazing up at it with concentration working his brow.

"This is the one?" Henry asked.

"I'm fairly certain." He indicated the front garden, so far overgrown it almost seemed to be disappearing back into the jungle. "She said it had an English garden. . . . I think I can see lavender in there."

Lavender. Faith's favorite flower. She had given him a sprig from her mother's garden the first time they met. The powdery smell of it always returned him to that moment, reminded him of her laughing eyes, her cool hands. . . .

"This is where she lived," he murmured, so quietly that

Howlett, who was making his way to the front door, didn't hear him.

He crossed the rutted road, mud sucking at his boots. An elderly native man worked on the veranda of the house next door, beating a rug rhythmically. It was loud in the hazy afternoon air—and seemed to echo the thump of Henry's heart.

Howlett was already knocking at the door, calling, "Halloo! You know, I think there's nobody home," he said to Henry.

Henry went to the window that looked on to the veranda. He rubbed the salt and dirt off it with the side of his fist and pressed his face up against the glass. A long-legged spider skittered away.

"You there! I say!" This was Howlett, using his awkward half-Sinhalese, half-English on the neighbor. Henry didn't need the neighbor to confirm it: the house was empty. Dust and a broken chair were the only objects in the front room. Paint peeled with the weight of too many humid summers; dirty strands of cobwebs hung along the cornices. He allowed himself a moment of self-pity, then told himself to be sensible. Just because she wasn't in this house any more, didn't mean he wouldn't find her.

Howlett returned from his conversation with the

neighbor. "She hasn't lived here for twelve years," he said. "The old man next door says she was here only four years, barely said a word to anyone, then went to live on a ship, the *Monkey King*. English, apparently. Do you know of it?"

"A ship? But she hated ships. At least . . . that's what she told me." He mused on this a moment. "Did the neighbor say anything else? Anything that can help us find her?"

Howlett scratched his head. "Truth be told, he was a little hard to understand, and he was very keen to convert us to some godforsaken pagan religion. Few words about ships, and far too many urging us to pray in one of those hideous temples. But the name of the ship was, at least, clear. We can write away to Colombo, for old shipping records."

Henry cheered himself. Shipping records, of course. They might be able to track down the owner of the *Monkey King*, and from there, discover where Faith was now.

"Thank you, Howlett," Henry said. "I shall draft a letter this afternoon."

———

Finally free of Orlando's chatter, Constance went to her room and lay down for a few moments on her bed, feet dangling off the side. On the trip into town, Orlanda had taken her to the stationer to order paper, ribbons and wax, and was now threatening to make her spend the next two days organizing guest lists and planning menus. Constance had pleaded a headache and escaped.

It was very warm in her bedroom now, as the western sun found her window. She closed her eyes and had the odd sensation of the phantom sea moving under her again. Father had said it might take a few days for her to reacquire her "land legs."

Father. He had been acting very strangely this afternoon on their walk home from town. She suspected he and Howlett had discovered something about her mother, because he was tight-lipped and distracted. Then he had shut himself in Howlett's library with a quick command to Chandrika to bring paper and ink. But what had they discovered?

She rose and paced to the window to close the shutters against the sun. She glanced down at the beach and saw Alexandre. He sat on the sand, a large drawing book across his lap, gazing out at the water. His shoulder was flexed towards her, and she was overcome by the desire to touch that shoulder, to feel his warm skin beneath the loose cotton shirt.

What was she thinking? These weren't thoughts that a young woman of her position, of her breeding, should be entertaining. But that was precisely the problem: Alexandre made her forget social position; he made her forget good manners and all the other polished surfaces of society. He made her feel the delicious naturalness of what lay beneath.

Constance sank back from the window, leaning her shoulder against the wall. It would do nobody any good to think such things. She pinched her own wrist, the sharp pain concentrating her senses on something other than Alexandre. When she moved away from the window, she took only one last glance.

Father was talking to him. He had sat on the sand next to Alexandre and was giving him instruction of some kind. She watched, curious, a few moments, feeling inexplicably guilty; as though they could both read her thoughts. Then it dawned on her. If Father was on the sand giving Alexandre instructions, he was no longer in Howlett's library making secret notes.

And she very much wanted to see what he suspected about her mother.

As she cracked open her bedroom door, she was most afraid of arousing Orlanda's attention. If her new friend found her creeping about, she wouldn't have a moment's peace.

Down the stairs she crept, stealthily, then dashed past the parlour and into the library. She closed the door behind her. The French doors to the garden were closed, and the room was stuffy. She glanced around and could see no writing paper, no ink well. The writing table nestled in the corner of the room was bare. He'd hidden what he was working on.

She began to search the bookshelves. Beneath a six-volume edition of Homer's *Odyssey*, she found a large flat stationery box. She removed the books, opened the box, and found a letter. It was much blotted. Only a draft. He hadn't known how to word it. Perhaps his walk on the beach was to clear his head, to make the words organize themselves better. If that was the case, he might be back soon. She scanned the letter quickly. It was to the registrar of the East India Company's shipping index in Colombo.

I wish to inquire about a ship named Monkey King, *suspected of English origin, known in the north-west of Ceylon in or about 1787. I have no information regarding class, size or purpose. I wish to know in whose name the ship was registered, and whether the Company has any further records that may apply, specifically if any of those records relate to a person named Faith Blackchurch. . . .*

Footsteps behind her. Her heart jumped. She turned. It was only Orlanda.

"What on earth are you doing down here?"

Constance quickly closed the lid of the box in her lap and picked up a volume of *The Odyssey*. "Reading," she said.

Orlanda came to take the volume off her, wrinkling her nose as she read the title. While she was distracted, Constance quietly slid the box back onto the shelf.

"You're reading Homer? Lord, really? I didn't think anybody actually read Homer. I thought they just bought his books because they looked impressive." Orlanda peered closely at the book.

Constance smiled, thinking of how Aunty Violet had insisted she read Homer and how Constance had, indeed, found it hard work.

"In any case, I thought you had a headache," Orlanda continued, somewhat skeptically.

"I do. But it was hot in my room."

"Ah! I told you so," said Orlanda, temporarily satisfied. "You'll have to ask your father to prevail upon mine. We could share a room." She strode to the French doors and opened them, letting a warm gust of sea air in. "Now, would you like to hear exciting news?"

Constance feigned interest. No doubt it would be about the dance. "Yes, of course."

"I've been speaking with my mother. I find that she's only too ready to comply with my requests at certain times of the day." Orlanda went into an exaggerated pantomime, lifting her trembling hand to her lips with an imaginary glass. "I've said I'd like to improve my French. I'm sure you can imagine why." Here she trailed off into a sly giggle. "A certain *French* boy that I've met has got me very interested."

Constance felt a stab of jealousy. She didn't answer.

"So, can you imagine what I've asked her? Oh, you'll love this. It is so wickedly perfect."

"What have you asked her?"

She began to laugh. "I've asked if Alexandre can come once a week to give us French lessons!" she squealed. "And the best part? She said yes!"

As the sun sank, the waves began to rush, and the day

began to cool. Orlanda had been called sternly by Howlett—a lack of attention to her daily chores was at issue—and Constance took the opportunity to let herself out of the library and through the garden to the colonnaded dancing room.

From there she picked her way over the sand to where Alexandre sat, alone.

She watched from a distance a few moments. Then he seemed to sense her presence and turned. He smiled.

"Good afternoon," she said.

"Good afternoon, Constance," he replied.

"I . . . ah . . . my father has been to see you?"

"Yes. Plans for the pearler."

He didn't invite her to sit with him, but of course he couldn't. Not really. It would be seen as inappropriate, even on this wide empty beach.

How little she cared for what was appropriate.

She sat next to him on the sand. His feet were bare, and she wished hers were too, so she could feel the warm sand between her toes. "I saw you from upstairs," she said, indicating the villa over her shoulder. "You were drawing."

"I like to draw."

"May I see?"

He reluctantly opened his drawing book and began to turn the pages. "These are all of *La Reine des Perles*," he said. "But these . . ." He trailed off, began flipping slowly through a series of pictures in the same place. Each was slightly different.

"They're beautiful. Where is this?"

"It is a place in France I saw when I was a boy. I do not know the name, but it is always in my mind. Like a pleasant dream. You wake and you want to go back. . . ."

"But you can never quite get there. I know." She turned her eyes to the sunset. Rose blush and dusty blue. Clouds across the horizon obscured the sun.

He seemed to read her thoughts. "The clouds ruin it. They always ruin it. I have watched hundreds of sunsets over the sea, and there are nearly always clouds on the horizon. Only three times have I seen the sun sink into the water unobscured. It is spectacular. A ball of flame extinguishing itself."

Constance loved the way he spoke, his soft accent. She fervently hoped that Orlanda's plan to have him in the villa once a week would work out, but knew in her heart that Father would object. He had very clear ideas about people's social situations. No matter how kindly he treated Alexandre, he believed crew belonged a long way from ladies and gentlemen.

"It's still beautiful. Even with the clouds," she said. The sea breeze tugged at her bonnet. "Alexandre, earlier today I . . . you said you would help me. With my search for my mother."

He turned to her, smiled slightly, as though afraid to smile completely. "Yes. Yes, of course."

"Her name was . . . is Faith Emilia Blackchurch. She went missing in 1782. All I know is that Father had enough reason to believe she might be here that he took out an empty ship to find her. There was a ship, I think. The *Monkey King*. You speak the local language. If you can find out anything—anything at all, no matter how small it might seem—I'd be so grateful."

"I will do my best."

They fell into silence as the sun slipped behind the horizon and the blue twilight came. Finally, Alexandre stretched his legs. "I had best get back aboard my vessel, before it is too dark."

"I suppose it's nearly supper time."

He stood and held out a hand to help her to her feet. She took it, heart in her mouth. His skin was warm, rough. He released her fingers as soon as she was on her feet, but she thought she sensed reluctance. Her blood fluttered in her veins.

"Goodnight, Alexandre," she said.

"Goodnight."

Then she returned to the villa. The soft evening air was heavy with the smell of spice and smoke. She felt warm, as though she had been told a secret, or made a promise. Her feet were light on the flagstones back towards the library.

Father was at the writing desk, a lantern newly lit beside him. He glanced up, then shoved his papers under his elbow and leapt to his feet.

"Constance, I hadn't thought to see you here."

"I've been for a stroll."

"On the sand. Yes, I see. You've brought in a trail on your shoes."

Constance looked behind her and saw the sand on Howlett's rug. "Oh," she said.

"Never mind. You can clean it up later. I have to talk to you."

She untied her bonnet, excitement filling her up. Was he going to share his search for Faith after all? "Have you heard something?"

His eyebrows drew down. "Yes, I have. And I don't like it at all."

Constance gulped, her heart frozen. "Oh, no! Is she dead?"

"Dead? Is *who* dead?"

"Mother."

"I wasn't speaking of your mother." Father uttered a sigh of exasperation, pacing away from her. "Constance, my business here is my own. I don't have a mind to share it."

Constance hardened her heart against him. *Fine,* she thought, *then I shan't share my business either, and we shall see who finds her first.*

"I'm referring to this nonsense about the French lad. Howlett's silly daughter—" He realized his voice was too loud and dropped it to a harsh whisper. "Orlanda has gained her mother's approval to have French lessons with him weekly. I think it is out of the question. I'm sure he's a nice boy, but he's crew. Crew don't teach ladies French. Let the Howletts put their daughter in harm's way. But not mine."

She didn't ask him what particular harm he thought Alexandre capable of. "But Father, you always urge me to continue my French instruction."

His eyes narrowed. "And you always tell me that you'd rather study astronomy. Why is French now so interesting?"

Constance retreated from the question. Any strenuous protests would draw suspicion. She feigned indifference. "It matters nothing to me," she said. "Orlanda can have lessons with him, and I shall enjoy the peace and quiet." Though she'd get little peace, being tortured by her own jealousy.

"Ah." Father pressed his lips together hard. "Well, there's the problem. I don't want to offend Howlett, nor his wife. If I forbid you, then it looks as though I am judging the way they are raising their daughter. They must be made to think it is your decision."

"Father," she said in a mock-shocked voice, "are you asking me to lie?"

"I am asking you to help me keep good friends on side."

"Orlanda will say that she won't take no for an answer. She'll probably sob with disappointment."

He turned his shoulder to her, idly spinning the mounted globe that sat on the mantelpiece. "Orlanda is a ninny. She'll soon recover."

A few moments of silence passed between them. Outside, crickets had started to chirp. "Is that all, Father?" Constance asked.

"That is all."

"I'll see you at supper then?"

He turned and met her gaze. "Constance, I don't understand young women, and I never have. But I must say this to you: I hope most fervently that you haven't developed ideas about Alexandre that are . . . not fitting."

She wanted to demand of him: *Why must I always fit?* Instead, she said, "No, Father. Of course not."

"Well. No good would come of it, you understand? Remember you are a civilized English woman, not a wild savage. Let Orlanda be foolish. You are a sensible girl."

Ordinarily, she would glow at his compliment; they were so rarely bestowed. But this time it was misplaced. She was, indeed, having thoughts about Alexandre that were far from sensible.

Chapter 10

An anxious knot sat in Alexandre's stomach the morning of the first French lesson. It had been a week since they had arrived at Nagakodi, and five days since Howlett had cornered him and told him that he would be instructing the "young ladies" in the library every Tuesday.

"You won't receive payment," Howlett said. "Acceptance into my home should be payment enough for a man of your social situation."

Alexandre would have accepted these terms anyway. But the prospect of being with Constance once a week made him agree readily, though he'd been careful not to appear too eager.

Today, too, he had information for her. He had questioned a number of the locals and discovered that Faith Blackchurch was remembered by many of them—and not for good reasons. She had lived locally for four years, gained a reputation for a cruel temper with the local traders, before disappearing. Getting Constance alone to speak to her, however, might prove difficult. Orlanda was very overbearing.

He brought the rowboat ashore and stepped out. He was unused to wearing shoes, and these were an old pair of de Locke's boots, too small for him. Still, he imagined he looked quite respectable: shod, hair tied back, buttons all fastened, cuffs unrolled and tight at his wrists. He walked up to the villa and knocked soundly on the front door.

Chandrika showed him in. Orlanda waited in the library with Howlett. Constance was nowhere in sight. Morning sunshine slanted into the room and illuminated the green leaves of the hibiscus outside the French doors.

Howlett unfolded his spidery body from the couch, glancing at his pocket watch. "Ah, you are punctual, I see."

A mixture of tension and confusion made him hold his tongue. He stood wordlessly, aware he should say something but not sure what it was.

"Good, then," Howlett muttered. "Orlanda, let the young man go after one hour. I shall come to check." He turned to Alexandre. "She hasn't much of a brain, so do be easy on her." Then he left.

Orlanda smiled at him prettily. "Sit here with me on the sofa."

"Where is Constance?" he said, without moving.

"Constance has been just beastly!" Orlanda said, her bottom lip pushed out. "She says she has no desire to learn French and wouldn't be persuaded to think otherwise—not even for me, her only friend in Ceylon! I am so very disappointed in her." She patted the seat next to her, all smiles again. "Come. Sit."

Alexandre did as she asked, all the time feeling the sink of his heart. When Constance had come to speak to him on the beach, he had been certain he saw some flicker of feeling in her eyes. He felt very deflated, foolish even. Orlanda was chattering to him without pause, but he couldn't bring himself either to listen or to respond.

"Shall we begin, Alexandre?" She handed him a piece of paper on which she had written a column of French words and phrases. "Here is a list I've made. Could you tell me how to pronounce them correctly?"

When he saw what they were, he was speechless.

"What's wrong?" she said. "Can you not read?"

"I . . . yes. I can read." De Locke had taught him to read, one of his only precious gifts. The problem was the nature of the words: *Love, she loves him, he loves her, I love you, you love me. Kiss, she kisses him, he kisses her, I kiss you, you kiss me.*

Her voice became hard. "Well, then, do as I ask."

Alexandre thought quickly and handed back the paper. "I can't read them as they are. The grammar is all wrong. I think for our first lesson we should concentrate on grammar."

Orlanda, temporarily foiled, put the list aside and paid close attention. "Yes," she said. "Let's start with *you*." Orlanda was not as dim-witted as her father thought. In fact, she was very bright. Her problem was that she couldn't focus for long without being distracted by some trivial thought or another, all of which she felt compelled to voice. Alexandre estimated half the lesson was idle chatter. He didn't mind listening to her, but he was not given much to talking, so he spent a lot of time in silence.

"Alexandre," she said, when he was certain that the hour must have already passed and had started to wonder if Howlett was going to come back to set him free, "I have something for you."

He was puzzled and, truth be told, a little concerned. "I beg your pardon?"

She slipped her hands behind her neck and released the clasp on the necklace she was wearing, a little gold bird on a chain.

Alexandre leaned away from her as she offered it to

him. "No, no," he said. "I cannot accept a gift from you."

"But I want you to have it." She reached for his hand, tried to prise open his fingers, and managed to tangle it around his thumb. All the while he protested and she insisted. Then the door to the room opened, and Orlanda jumped away as if scalded, leaving the necklace wrapped around Alexandre's fingers. Presuming it to be her father, he quickly thrust his hand into his pocket.

It wasn't her father. It was Constance.

"Good morning, dear friend," Orlanda said smoothly. "I'm sorry, but the French lesson is finished. It is too late for you to change your mind."

"I don't wish to change my mind. Good morning, Alexandre," she said, but he found he couldn't meet her eye. "Orlanda, the paper and ribbons have arrived from the stationer."

Orlanda squeaked. "Lovely! Now we can get on with making the invitations." She turned to Alexandre. "I'm going to host a dance, you see. Would you like—" Then she stopped herself, and an uncomfortable silence dragged out, as they all realized she had been about to invite him, then thought better of it.

"It's a very great shame, but I don't suppose I can invite

him," Orlanda said, turning to Constance, who had the decency to blush. "Father will expect me to invite only ladies and gentlemen. Do you think I should ask if I can make an exception?"

Alexandre wavered between embarrassment and anger. His pride made him speak up. "I do not wish to go," he said. "Such a gathering does not interest me."

"Yes, I imagine you would be very uncomfortable," Orlanda continued, still oblivious to the embarrassment she may have caused him. "I expect you don't even know the simplest dance. We shall have to manage without you, shan't we, Constance?"

Constance examined her hands, refusing to meet Orlanda's eyes. Orlanda bustled to the door. "Thank you for today's lesson, Alexandre," she said. "Can I show you to the door?"

Alexandre stood and pointed his thumb behind him. "May I go through the garden? It's quicker."

"But I have to collect my stationery at the front door," she said.

"I'll show him out," Constance offered.

Orlanda looked at her, narrowed her eyes fractionally, then shrugged. "Certainly." She flounced off, leaving Constance and Alexandre alone in the library.

"This way," she said, moving ahead of him. There was such grace in her movements, not like Orlanda's overly cultured primness. As they passed through the French doors into the garden, she dropped her voice to a whisper and said, "Have you any news of my mother?"

Alexandre felt a wave of irritation, and tried to understand its cause. Perhaps it was that she had not considered him good enough to teach her French; and yet now, when she needed something from him, she was not averse to his company. The baffling thing to Alexandre was why any of this mattered. He had never in his life cared what people thought of him, of his social situation. But with Constance, he cared very much.

"Alexandre?" she said, stopping and turning to him. "Did you hear my question?"

He shook off these feelings, more fitting for a silly girl like Orlanda. "Yes, Constance. A number of people remember her."

Constance's eyes rounded. "They do?"

"Yes, and they told me where she once lived. But she is no longer there." She had gone pale, and he had to resist the urge to reach out and take her hand. "Are you well?"

"I'm . . . it's just such a shock, I suppose. Nobody knows where she went?"

He shook his head, not telling her that many had thought the town well rid of her. "The house still stands, though, on the outer rim of the town, nearly in the jungle. I can tell you how to get there."

She nodded slowly. "Yes," she said, "yes, there might be something there. A clue. A diary . . . something. But, Alexandre, could you take me there? If it's a long way from town, I should be quite nervous to go alone."

Complex emotions swam through him. The desire to be with her, to protect her, was strong. Much stronger than the insult he had felt at her imagined rejection. Despite his misgivings, he said softly, "I am at your service, Constance."

She chewed her lip, eyes turned skywards. "How are we to manage this? Orlanda is worse than a team of spies."

"I will be on the beach most afternoons at sunset. It is the time of day I most favor for drawing. For thinking. Come and find me when you can."

She smiled, brilliantly. It seemed the sun shined right through to his ribs. "I will. Thank you. Thank you." Then she was backing away, returning to the villa. He pulled off his uncomfortable boots and made his way down the beach to his boat.

It was only much later that he remembered the golden bird Orlanda had given him. Guiltily, he pulled it out of his pocket and hung it on a nail. Orlanda would likely not accept its return without much discomfort. He would decide what to do with it another time.

Days sped by and Constance began to think she would never get away to see Alexandre. Every afternoon, he sat on the beach to watch the sunset. She could see him from her window, and she watched the clouds gather on the horizon and hoped to be able to join him soon. But there was always something to constrain her: Orlanda with endless requests to help with guest lists and invitations; Father frowning at her sternly with reminders that she behave herself; even Chandrika, who caught her one afternoon just as she was heading out, to tell her that the cook had supper ready early and to be back within an hour. One hour wasn't enough!

Within a few days, she had hatched a plan. She went down to the library late one afternoon and found her father.

"Father?"

He turned. He had been writing a letter. She wondered

if it had something to do with her mother. "Yes, child?"

"I'm unwell."

He rose, came towards her, and put his palm across her forehead. "You're not feverish."

"I have a stomach ache, and I feel very tired."

"Do you want me to send for Burchfield?"

She shook her head. "I think I'd like to miss supper and go straight to bed. Only, could you make sure Orlanda doesn't get it in her head to look in on me? I'd like to sleep."

"Of course. I'll tell Chandrika." He smiled conspiratorially. "Because Lord knows, neither of her parents can control her."

She felt guilty as she made her way back up to her room. Father trusted her. She had to make doubly sure that he never found out where she was going this evening. And with whom.

In her room, she waited until she smelled the rich odor of soup fill the house and Chandrika called everybody to supper. She cracked open her door and listened. When she was certain everyone was in the dining room, she removed her shoes and crept down the stairs. Tiptoeing, she stuck close to the walls and made her way into the library and out into the garden.

She ran across the flagstones and out onto the beach,

laughter bubbling in her throat. She did it! She got away from all of them. The sand was warm between her toes. She scanned the beach for Alexandre and saw him a distance off putting his things back in the boat.

"Alexandre!" she called, then realized she shouldn't be calling so loud.

He glanced up and saw her. She waved madly. He raised his hand in return, then walked up the empty beach to greet her.

"Is it too late?" she said, panting from her run.

He looked over his shoulder at the water. "I expect I can find my vessel in the dark. Either that, or I can sleep on the beach tonight."

"Oh, not on my behalf! You mustn't sleep outside."

"Have you never slept outside? It's glorious. Especially in these warm parts of the world." He waved his hand dismissively. "I don't mind. I should like to take you to see your mother's house."

"Thank you," she said, catching her breath. "You can probably guess that nobody knows I'm out here, so we mustn't go back through Howlett's garden."

"There's a track through the trees," he said. "But you have no shoes."

"Nor do you."

"My feet are used to the ground, they're tough as leather."

"I took them off to sneak out." She looked over her shoulder at the villa, tall and ghostlike in the twilight. "I can't go back and get them." She met Alexandre's gaze again. "I'll be fine, I'm sure."

"Keep an eye out for rocks," he said, leading her up the beach and across the verge of tough grass, then in amongst the coconut palms.

The sun had almost slipped behind the world, and the trees crowded out the remaining light.

Constance kept her eyes fixed on the track in front of her, not just to avoid rocks, but also to stop herself from stealing glances at Alexandre, who seemed immensely close even though he walked four feet away from her. The misunderstanding about the dance haunted her: Orlanda's bumbling attempts to explain why she couldn't invite him, then Alexandre's fiery pride flaring into life (thrilling her heart, if truth be told). He didn't want to go, of course. Though she wished very much that he did, that Orlanda could convince her parents to invite him, just so Constance could have one dance with him, feel his warm arms, be close to his lean frame. She wanted to tell him that her father had made her stay away from the

French lessons, but didn't want to embarrass him again with mention of their social differences.

"When we get to the end of this track, we'll come out on the southern edge of the town. Quite close to where we need to go," he said.

"Will we be able to find it in the dark?"

"It's not dark yet," he said, indicating the twilight sky. "We'll find it."

The town was very different at this time of the day. The stalls were empty, and there was a jumble of traders packing their wares while their children played on the cobbled ground around them.

All the European settlers were at their homes for supper, and it seemed the area had been reclaimed by its former owners, who smiled and talked while they worked. Exotic cooking smells permeated the air. One or two people put their heads up to look at Constance and Alexandre as they crossed the corner of the square, but nobody called out or told them that it wasn't fitting for them to be seen together. It made Constance feel light of heart, light of step.

Until she cracked her toe on a protruding cobblestone.

"Ow!" she shouted, stopping and bending over to clutch her foot.

"What happened? Let me see," Alexandre said, crouching and gently pushing her hand away.

"Oh, oh, it hurts," she said, trying to be brave but failing.

"It's bleeding," he said. "Wait here. Sit down." He took her hand and helped her to sit on the ground. She tried not to think about how dirty her dress would get. He ran off towards the markets and began speaking to a young woman packing up a stall that sold brightly dyed cotton fabric. She glanced over at Constance with sympathy, then offered Alexandre a strip of rag.

He sat beside Constance and gently wrapped her toe, all the while speaking calmly. "It's a small cut so you aren't to worry. But I think you should go home. We'll be on muddy tracks. . . ."

"I can't go home," she said, wanting to sob. "It's been impossible to get away. . . ."

He stood and helped her to her feet, smiling. "I can carry you on my back."

"Oh, no, that won't be necessary," she said, even though she wanted to sigh, "Yes."

"I insist." He crouched in front of her.

She took a deep breath, then leaned forward, clasping her arms around his neck. He stood; the world fell away from her feet. He hooked his arms under her knees and her skirts rode up to her ankles. A sea breeze kissed her cheeks; her heart thumped wildly. He was so warm and so strong. She felt alive, more real than she had ever felt. She thought of her father's warning—that she remember she was civilized, an English woman—and wanted to laugh.

"Not far now," he said, picking his way down a rutted track. "Hold on tight."

She wanted to hold on forever. "I will," she breathed, not sure if he heard her.

The peculiar chatter and squeal of jungle animals reached her ears, and a rich damp smell rose, neither pleasant nor unpleasant, rather like dirt and rain and leaves rotten after too many seasons on the ground. Alexandre finally stopped in front of an overgrown garden, a house in darkness. He let her down, and she put her disappointed feet on the ground once again.

"Thank you," she said.

He smiled, slightly out of breath. "You are a tall girl, Constance."

Her heart fell. Did he think her a great lunk of a thing? Not like compact little Orlanda.

"But very graceful," he muttered, so she almost didn't hear it. A thrill fluttered through her, but he had turned and was eyeing the front of the house. "Shall we see if we can get inside?"

They tried the front door but it was locked, so they made their way around the side of the house, through prickling overgrown grass—she tried not to think of snakes—and to the back windows. Alexandre pried one open and climbed in. Constance hitched her skirts and climbed in after him, tearing her dress on the way.

"Oh, dear," she said, tying a hasty knot in it. "I'm afraid women aren't designed for this kind of adventure."

"I think it's women's clothes that are the problem," he said. "Not women themselves." Then he turned away, moving into the house. "Though I cannot imagine Orlanda dealing with the situation as capably as you."

She shone: a double pleasure in both a compliment to her and a denial of feelings for Orlanda.

They went through the house, room by room, hands clasped together tightly. Only a few items of furniture were left behind, and those were broken or bent. Then they came to a dark, windowless room where the skittering of little feet in the ceiling gave Constance pause.

"There's something here," Alexandre said, dropping her hand. "A piece of furniture, a desk. Shall I drag it out into the moonlight?"

"Please."

Together they hauled the old writing desk beneath a window. With shaking fingers, Constance dislodged all its drawers and felt beneath them. It was too easy to imagine some letter, full of import, hidden precisely for her. But there was nothing.

She fought with her disappointment as, covered in dust and sticky cobwebs, she climbed back out the window and into the balmy night air. Her excitement seemed to be slipping away. Once they stood outside in the long grass again, Alexandre considered her carefully.

"I'm sorry we didn't find anything."

"It was foolish to raise my hopes."

"There's a house next door to this one. Shall we go and ask them if they know anything?"

She shook her head. "It's a waste of time."

He hid a smile. "Ah, the English and their melancholia." He beckoned. "Come, Constance."

He led her back to the road, then up to the front door of the neighboring house. A dim light within told them somebody was home. Alexandre knocked and called out a Sinhalese word. A few moments later the door opened, and there stood an elderly woman with grey streaked hair and a shining jewel nestled in the side of her nose.

Alexandre greeted her and began to speak to her in Sinhalese. She was guarded, but answered all his questions nonetheless, spreading her hands for emphasis. Constance waited, feeling useless. A mosquito settled on her cheek; she slapped at it but missed. Night was truly upon them now, the half-moon bright in the sky. The jungle noise was almost deafening, now that the crickets had taken up their full voices.

Finally, Alexandre turned away and the woman went inside.

"What did she say?"

"She knew your mother."

Constance smiled. "Really? Did she like her? Were they friends?"

Alexandre glanced away. "No, not friends. Your mother lived alone and rarely spoke to anybody. But this woman remembers her going away, as you said, on a ship. An English ship, the *Monkey King*."

"That's what Father knows already," she muttered. "He must have been here before us. Did she say anything else?"

"She tells me there is a saying amongst the locals, and she has always wondered if it is about your mother. 'The English faith is in the hidden temple of Ranumaran.'"

"The English faith? My mother's name was Faith . . . I know it's almost too much to hope, but do you think it might be about her?"

"Even if it is, where is the hidden temple of Ranumaran?"

Constance turned these thoughts over in her head, constructing a complex fantasy. Her mother, abducted from her home in England, brought to Ceylon, then escaping on an English ship and finding herself in a holy place, one of the mysterious and beautiful Buddhist pagodas. And waiting there ever since, in hopes that her husband and daughter might come to find her. There were many lapses of common sense in the fantasy, but it was so compelling to Constance's heart that she couldn't help but cling to the hope. "As likely as it may be, I've got to try it."

"What?"

"How would we find Ranumaran?"

"Ask the locals, look at maps . . . I can help you."

"Would you? I'm certain my father knows nothing of this. His letter to the shipping registrar made no mention of Ranumaran."

"You should tell him."

She brushed away another mosquito. "No, I won't. He

thinks I'm young and foolish. If I can find Mother before he does, he will have to take me seriously."

"Perhaps he will." Alexandre considered her in the dark. "You should get back home."

Reluctantly, she agreed.

—•—

As she returned through the garden, Alexandre's goodnight still soft in her ears, she noticed a light burning in the library. She stood behind the stone post and peered out. It was Father, writing. She couldn't go in the front door without being seen, but she could hardly go into the library looking as she did: a bloody bandage on her bare feet, mud and dust on her dress, a rip in her skirt, mosquito bites on her hands and face. Especially as she was supposed to be sick in bed. She sighed, sagging into the post. What now?

She couldn't stay here outside the library; Father might see her. So she let herself into adjoining the spice garden, found a patch of soft grass under a cinnamon tree, and lay down.

The stars were a bright dust above her. She began organizing them into constellations—Procyon in Canis Minor, Sirius in Canis Major. Then she stopped and let them scatter again into their own random beauty.

She smiled. The air was warm and balmy, the sea beat rhythmically in the distance, and the scents of the spice garden were heady. She closed her eyes, turning over the events of the evening in her head. Alexandre, the old house, the clue to her mother's whereabouts. Then her thoughts began to skip and slip, and she drifted off into a sleep full of images of Alexandre.

Chandrika found her at dawn.

"Miss Blackchurch?"

Constance opened her eyes, remembered where she was, and sat up. The first words to her lips were, "Don't tell my father."

Chandrika smiled, her dark eyes shining. "If you only knew how often I have heard that from Orlanda." She took Constance's hand in her soft fingers. "Come. Everyone is still asleep. I am certain you can wash and change into clean clothes without being discovered."

"Thank you, thank you," Constance muttered, leaving the soft morning and all its exotic dreams behind her.

On the fifth day, a ship finally saw de Locke and sent a boat across for him.

By this stage, he had gone beyond anger to blind fury.

At every hunger pang, every interruption of his sleep, every quaver of fear at the sounds from the jungle, he muttered Alexandre's name with murderous intent.

It was an English ship, and for once he blessed the English. Because they might know where Blackchurch was. "I'm looking for a ship named *Good Bess*," he asked every crew member, until one finally said that he knew Henry Blackchurch, and that he most often did business with the East India Company in Colombo or Madras. The fact that de Locke had encountered him on the western side of Adam's Bridge indicated that Ceylon was his destination. The ship he was on was to sail to Colombo after a short stop in Tuticorin. De Locke had to make a decision. From Tuticorin, it was only a day's journey home. Should he just return, buy a new vessel, find a new crew. . . .?

The thought filled him with rage. No. He would not go home until this business was finished.

Chapter 11

Alexandre was small again, in a skinny boy's body, shivering in midnight air. The horse show was over; all the visitors had gone home. One grim light flickered nearby; the tank waited.

"I don't want to go in!" he protested. His heart threatened to burst through his ribs. Whispering shadows snaked around him.

"You shall go in." It was de Locke, pistol pointed at him. "You have no choice."

He climbed into the cold water. It tasted like the sea. He looked around and realized that he wasn't in the tank at all, but at the pearl banks. Nighttime, blue shadows, cruel-toothed creatures circling. De Locke pushed his head down. Alexandre struggled against him, but couldn't move. Crushed under the weight of the water, he fought to breathe. . . .

Alexandre woke with a jolt. Then relief flooded through him. It was a dream, nothing more.

He estimated from the position of the sun outside the round window that it was around eight o'clock. That meant he had an hour before he had to be at the Howletts' villa for Orlanda's French lessons. He turned on his side in his hammock and closed his eyes. Still, he couldn't completely dispel the anxiety that the dream had aroused. De Locke was a dangerous man, but he had always been on Alexandre's side. Now that he knew Alexandre had withheld a pearl from him, had jumped on the first passing ship . . .

He rose and dressed well enough to visit the villa. He had to speak to Henry Blackchurch.

Chandrika showed him into the drawing room, where Howlett and Blackchurch were deep in conversation. They looked up on his arrival. Howlett frowned, checking his pocket watch. "Are you not a little early, boy?"

"I hoped to speak with Captain Blackchurch," he said.

"Speak then," Blackchurch said.

"Sir, the *Queen of Pearls* is ready for sale. I wonder how long you imagine it will be before you have a buyer?"

"Keen to get home are you, Alexandre?" Blackchurch said with a tight smile. "My business here doesn't go so well. It might be some time. If nothing else, I have to wait until after this silly dance that our silly daughters have their hearts set upon."

Alexandre knew what Blackchurch's business was, of course. Constance had told him everything. "I think you misunderstand my meaning, Captain," he said. "When the pearler is sold, I will be able to move onto *Good Bess*. That is my aim. I don't mind how long we are anchored, but I have . . . doubts about my safety aboard de Locke's vessel alone."

"It's not de Locke's vessel," he snapped. "It's mine."

Howlett put a hand over his lips to stifle a laugh. "Doubts about your safety? You think this de Locke character would bother to come and hunt down a pearl diver?"

"I worked at his side for seven years; I know him very well," Alexandre said, deliberately keeping his voice cool. "If he finds me, he will punish me."

Howlett shook his head condescendingly, but Blackchurch was gentler. "Boy, your imagination has got the better of you. De Locke won't find us. I brought no cargo with me, the voyage is unregistered, and nobody knows I'm here. He will no doubt be angry with both of us. But he is a coward, and he will eventually creep home to lick his wounds."

His kindness brought Alexandre to his senses. Blackchurch was right: the nightmare had made his imagination run away with him. "Thank you, sir," he said.

"You can move aboard *Good Bess* if you wish, and I'll send another of my men to replace you on the pearler. But you won't find it quite so pleasant under the forecastle."

Alexandre considered. On *La Reine des Perles* he had his own space, independence, air to breathe. Reassured by the captain's words, he shook his head. "No, sir, I think I will stay where I am."

"I'm glad to hear it. I have sent a letter to the pearl fisheries superintendent and hope to have him find a buyer in the next few weeks. Hopefully before I sail for England. And don't worry, I have warned him about de Locke and told him not to divulge our whereabouts."

"Thank you, sir."

"Run along, now, boy," Howlett said. "No doubt Orlanda will be on her way to meet you in the library."

Alexandre sighed inwardly. Ah, yes, much safer than dealing with de Locke, but no less frightening. French lessons with Orlanda.

———

When Constance heard a great thumping and a flurry of raised voices, she decided to go downstairs to investigate. Especially as one of those raised voices was Orlanda's.

"No, no," she shouted. "I said out there."

Constance came through the library and into the garden to see two local men struggling with the clavichord, while Orlanda pointed and gestured furiously.

"What's going on?" Constance asked.

"I'm trying to get these two dunderheads to move our clavichord out to the dancing room, in readiness for the dance."

"But the dance isn't for over a week."

"I like to be prepared."

Constance moved towards the group and placed a firm hand on the clavichord, indicating the men should put it down.

They did so. One wiped the sweat from his forehead on his shoulder.

"Orlanda," Constance said slowly, "the dancing room is not fully enclosed. If we have a storm, the clavichord will get wet."

"Oh," she said. "I hadn't thought of that. Perhaps I should leave it until next week then." She blew noisily. "It's such a disappointment, Constance. Father won't hire musicians, so I have to rely on Mother to play the clavichord and if she's had too much of her medicine she will make a terrible mess of it." She looked at the large instrument, sitting half on the flagstones and half on the grass, and sighed. "Well, then. You'd better put this back in the house, and I had better impress upon Mother the importance of daily practice."

The men looked at her, puzzled.

"Back in the . . ." She began to gesture again, then grew fed up. "Oh, why haven't you bothered to learn English, for goodness' sake?"

Constance didn't point out that Orlanda hadn't bothered to learn Sinhalese. "Would you like me to get Chandrika?" she offered.

"Please. I'm having a devil of a time with these two. I shall tell Father to pay them only half, for indeed they only got the clavichord halfway to the dancing room."

Constance smiled at the men, but they didn't smile back, no doubt judging her as harshly as they judged Orlanda. She felt embarrassed to be English and determined to learn a few basic words while she was here. *Please* and *thank you* would be a start. "I'll find Chandrika," she said, and hurried into the house.

Chandrika was in the laundry, running a towel through the mangler.

"Orlanda needs you to translate," Constance said. "Do you have a moment?"

"Of course," she answered, wiping her wet hands on her apron.

It suddenly occurred to Constance that Chandrika might know of the place her mother was supposed to be. "Chandrika," she said slowly. "Do you know of the hidden temple of Ranumaran?"

"Ranumaran? It is a fishing village about twenty miles north of here. But I know of no temple there. Though, if it is hidden. . ." She smiled, and Constance had to laugh.

"My sister's husband is from Ranumaran," Chandrika continued. "He would know. He lives on the northern side of town. I am going to see them next Thursday, if you would like to come."

Next Thursday, a week away. The waiting would tie her stomach in knots. Constance needed to know before then.

"Or I could just give you his address. His English is quite good."

"That would be wonderful. How do you say thank you in Sinhalese?"

"*Istuti.*"

"*Istuti*, Chandrika."

"*Nalladu varuka*, Constance. You're welcome."

Constance's feet, scratched and scabbed, had suffered in shoes for too long that day. She had them up on her pillow, wiggling her toes. She quickly threw the covers over them when Orlanda flounced in that afternoon, brandishing a piece of paper.

"Look!" she said, flopping onto Constance's bed. As she did so, Constance's feet were uncovered, and Orlanda recoiled dramatically. "Dear Lord! What happened to you?"

Constance's pulse thudded quickly in her throat. "I . . . was on the beach and I kicked a rock. Didn't see it."

Orlanda frowned. "I've lived here rather a long time and never seen a rock on our beach."

"A little further up," Constance tried. "The ocean end." She indicated Orlanda's sheet of paper, hoping to distract her. "Is this our guest list?"

Constance's feet were forgotten. "Yes!" Orlanda squealed. Is it not exciting? Twenty-five people are coming!"

"We really must think about decorating the dancing room very soon. Only your point about the rain is a good one." Orlanda suddenly went white, her cold fingers grasping Constance's wrist.

"No! What if it rains on the night of the dance?"

"It's not worth worrying about, Orlanda. Even you can't control the elements."

Orlanda fixed Constance in her gaze. "Sometimes I think you don't take me seriously."

Constance gave her a squeeze. "Come, show me the list."

The guests were drawn from all the European settlers in the near vicinity, plus ship's officers at anchor, mostly Dutch and English. "But look," Orlanda said, pointing out one of the names, "Madame *et* Monsieur Croix. They're French. I shall no doubt impress them with my command of their tongue."

Constance couldn't stop herself from asking about Alexandre. She hadn't spoken to him since their adventure two nights ago, and every day that went by without him was dull and colorless. "How are your lessons progressing?" she asked.

"They would be better if Alexandre taught me what I wanted to know, rather than endless grammar."

"What do you want to know?"

Orlanda smiled impishly and shook her head. "You are all of a sudden very interested for somebody who declared herself averse to learning French at all."

Constance let it go, moving to the window. She could see Alexandre's boat, making its way to shore. Ready to watch the sunset.

Climbing out her window and jumping the thirty feet to the beach would be easier than getting past Orlanda. There was simply no question of telling her she was going for a walk alone on the beach and escaping. Orlanda would want to come. But Constance needed to see Alexandre alone, to ask him to come with her to speak with Chandrika's brother-in-law.

Unexpected help came, at that moment, in the form of a burst of fumbled music: Mrs. Howlett had sat down at the clavichord in the drawing room.

"What on earth is . . . ?" Orlanda sat up, pressing her hands into her temples. "Is that a quadrille? Oh, my, the rhythm is completely wrong. She'll ruin everything!" In a second, she was on her feet and out the door.

Constance knew that she had no time to waste. She gave Orlanda one minute to get to the drawing room, then raced out of her room and outside. She knew that, in ten minutes, Orlanda would come looking for her, but she hoped that within ten minutes she and Alexandre would be on their way to town.

"Hello," she said, stopping on the sand next to him.

He looked up and put his drawing book aside. "More clouds," he said, gesturing to the horizon. "I told you so."

She spoke quickly and breathlessly. "Chandrika's brother-in-law comes from Ranumaran. His name is Nissanka. I'm going to see him right now."

"Do you need me to come?"

She decided to be honest. "I might not *need* you. Chandrika says his English is good. But I'd like you to come. Just in case." She glanced behind her at the villa. "But we'll need to be quick because Orlanda is probably noticing I'm not where she left me, right now."

Alexandre smiled, and scrambled to his feet. "Straight through to the track then," he said. "And I'm glad to see you're wearing shoes this time."

In his company, she felt herself light up again, as though all her senses now stood alert. As they walked, their hands sometimes brushed close to each other, creating sparks of heat. When his hand picked up hers briefly to lead her off the path into town, her body had a complex and entirely new reaction. Her stomach hollowed out, her knee bones melted away, and her face grew hot.

He dropped her hand as soon as they entered the market square, but still she couldn't stop herself from smiling.

They found Nissanka's house on a rutted street just outside town, one of a dozen *cadjan* houses, made of timber and woven coconut palm leaves. A woman—Constance surmised this was Chandrika's sister—sat outside on an old wooden chair in the long shadows of afternoon, watching as three small children played on the thick grass.

"Hello," Constance said, approaching. "Chandrika sent me. I wanted to speak with Nissanka."

At the mention of her sister's name, the woman smiled and rose. She spoke in rapid Sinhalese, which Alexandre translated. "She says welcome and asks after Chandrika."

"Tell her she's well. Is her husband home?"

More translating passed, and it transpired that she was waiting for Nissanka to return from fishing, that he was expected any moment. She invited them in for tea, which they accepted.

Constance and Alexandre sat at a plain wooden table under the low roof, while Chandrika's sister—her name was Sirimavo—boiled water on the fire and made aromatic tea from fresh leaves. The children continued calling to each other outside in the gathering dusk, and Constance started to worry that soon she would be missed at the villa. Orlanda's questions didn't worry her; but her father's did. She drank her tea—very rich and sweet—and felt the tick of every second in the tight space under her ribs.

Finally, Nissanka arrived home with a string of fish. He handed them to Sirimavo and looked curiously at her guests.

"Hello, I'm Constance," Constance said, rising and offering him her hand. "Chandrika said you might speak to me. She says you come from Ranumaran."

He nodded slowly. "I grew up there. But I live here in Nagakodi long time now." He sat at the table, and Sirimavo rose to make him tea as well.

Constance returned to her seat. "We want to know the location of a place called the hidden temple of Ranumaran."

His puzzled expression told her that he hadn't understood, so Alexandre translated. Nissanka shook his head. "I am sorry; I have never hear of any temple in Ranumaran. There is Bodhi tree where they gather on *poya* days, but it is not . . . what was the word you say?"

"Hidden?" Constance prompted.

"No, it not *hidden*."

Constance fought with her disappointment.

"Next week I go to visit my mother there," Nissanka continued. "You want me ask her? Ask others?"

"If you would. I'd appreciate it," Constance said. "*Istuti.*"

He smiled, and corrected her pronunciation.

"I had better go," she said to Alexandre.

Alexandre thanked Sirimavo and Nissanka in Sinhalese, and he and Constance hurried back into town. It was on the path back through to the beach that they ran into her father.

"Father!" she said, flushing guiltily, glad that Alexandre hadn't taken her hand again.

"Constance, where have you been? Orlanda said you went missing over an hour ago." His eyes turned to Alexandre. "And what are you doing with one of my crew?"

"I found Miss Blackchurch at the markets," he lied smoothly. "I was showing her this quick way home, as she was worried about the coming dark."

"What were you doing at the markets, Constance?" he asked.

She thought quickly. Father expected her to be vain and silly, so she said, "Looking for something new and pretty to wear to the dance. I only brought three dresses with me, and they are getting very worn."

Father turned to Alexandre with a suspicious drawing-down of his eyebrows. "You can go. I'll accompany Constance home."

"Goodnight, Miss Blackchurch, Captain," he said politely, going ahead of them.

Father waited until Alexandre was gone before taking Constance's elbow and leading her forward. "Since when have you thought it sensible to go out and buy a dress right on supper time?"

"I didn't buy anything," she said. "I was just looking at materials."

"Answer my question. You know better, and I know that you know better."

She blinked back at him, not sure what to say. The sea breeze rattled the palm leaves all around. "Orlanda," she said. "She's suffocating me. I needed to get away from her."

The tension in his body seemed to shift. He was still angry, but now he understood. "Ah. I can imagine. Still, running around at nighttime is not the answer. If you need to be away from her, you may come and sit with me in the library. I am helping Howlett with his paperwork, and I spend many hours there in the afternoons. You could read a book. It would be far too dull for Orlanda's taste."

Constance's mind reeled in trying to comprehend the difference between sitting silently in the library with Father and running about in the open air with Alexandre, but she nodded anyway. "Thank you, Father. Perhaps I shall."

He took her hand and squeezed it, his voice dropping quietly. "Don't disappear like that again, Constance."

"I won't," she said, not meaning it.

"It reminds me of . . ." He shook his head. "Let's not speak of it any more. Our supper is waiting."

As they returned home, she realized what he had been about to say. *It reminds me of . . .* He was speaking of the night her mother disappeared, and she felt such strong guilt that it almost brought tears to her eyes. She had made him worry; she had made him think it was all happening again. She almost told him everything: how Alexandre was helping her, how she was finding out about the hidden temple of Ranumaran. But she held back. If he knew, he would make her stay home, never see Alexandre again. So she fell silent at his side, feeling sorry for him for the first time in her life.

Chapter 12

The sea breeze caught the long trailing paper streamers that Constance and Orlanda were twining about the columns and roofbeams of the dancing room. Orlanda had complained that the space was "drab and much in need of decoration." Constance thought the breathtaking view out across the harbor, and the deep garden, was anything but drab. But Orlanda was impossible to disagree with. So they wrapped and tied the streamers— Constance standing on a chair to reach the higher places —while Orlanda chattered *endlessly* about nothing of consequence. Constance had learned to make interested noises even though she wasn't listening any more, her thoughts rambling off over the water. Her mother, the hidden temple of Ranumaran, Alexandre . . .

Alexandre. She realized his name had been spoken aloud. She turned to Orlanda.

"What did you say, Orlanda?"

Orlanda stood back from a pillar, tying the streamer's

end. "Really, Constance, are you deaf? I said, Father has decided to ask Alexandre to be a footman at the dance. He says the settlers in the area are tired of seeing natives in service, so he thought it would add a touch of class to the night." She unraveled another streamer, yellow this time. "I dare say he's right. You know, footmen are supposed to be tall, imposing . . . handsome." Then she dropped her voice to a tone that was, for Orlanda, almost thoughtful. "It will be nice to have him there. I've grown rather fond of him."

Constance stopped hanging streamers and eyed Orlanda carefully. Her friend looked up coyly, a mischievous smile on her lips. Constance's jealousy made it difficult for her to speak. "Orlanda, what are you thinking?"

"Well, I'm not going to shout it to you up there."

Constance climbed down from the chair and came to stand by Orlanda, who gave her another roll of colored paper. Together, they began wrapping the same pillar.

Orlanda spoke conspiratorially, her voice nearly washed away by the sound of the sea. "I have come to know Alexandre over the past few weeks, and I find him most agreeable company. I am almost certain he feels the same way. Constance," she grasped Constance's hand, "I love him. Most ardently."

"But . . . but . . ." Constance found her voice. "There are so many impediments," she managed. "There is no possibility of a match." Speaking those words aloud made her feel sad, bereft. But not for Orlanda's sake.

"Do you not think that love can overcome anything? Did Shakespeare not say, 'Let me not to the marriage of true minds admit impediment'?"

Love. Orlanda was in love with Alexandre. Why did the thought make Constance feel short of breath, anxious, as though she wanted to cry? Jealousy harder than diamonds tightened inside her.

"Do you need me to remind you, Orlanda?" Constance said. "He is in service to my father. You are the daughter of a gentleman. When was there ever a match made under such circumstances?"

"He is only in service to your father temporarily. Don't forget he also teaches me French. Why, a friend of my cousin in Oxfordshire married his governess. It's quite common."

"For a man to marry a woman of lower social standing, yes. But I have never seen the opposite, Orlanda. Never."

Orlanda's voice became increasingly whining. "Our fathers are not so very genteel. They have property, certainly, but they are in trade. They have no titles to protect, no ancient families to please. Alexandre is perfectly nice. I know he has rough edges, but he could be trained to be a gentleman: converse appropriately, learn how to dance, wear shoes . . ."

Constance bristled. To think Orlanda had almost invited Alexandre to the dance as a guest, but was now pleased for him to go as a servant. To think that she had declared love for him, but also spoke of him as though he were a puppy to be taught tricks. Her words came out savagely. "You are deluding yourself. Your father will never allow you to form an attachment to Alexandre; it would cause him extreme dishonor. Love counts for naught when you're English, Orlanda. All that counts is appearance. You are a lady and, one day, you will marry a gentleman. Whether you like him or not. And you are a little fool to think otherwise." She stopped, realizing her heart was beating rapidly, that tears were just a blink away.

Orlanda, who had been shocked into uncustomary silence, finally found her tongue. "You speak very passionately, friend. But is your warning directed at me, or at yourself?"

Constance handed Orlanda the roll of paper. "I feel unwell," she said. "I must—"

"Go," Orlanda finished for her. "You're unwell and

you must go. I know that you are not unwell, Constance. I know that you pretend to be unwell because my company is so tedious to you. I can only presume that my dullness is the reason my father is always at work, and my mother is always indisposed with her medicine."

Constance softened. "Orlanda, I—"

Orlanda turned her shoulder. "I wouldn't keep you here a moment past endurance. Go."

Constance pinched the bridge of her nose, her mind in turmoil. Then she turned and escaped to the beach.

The midday sun stood directly overhead, hot on her skin. She wasn't wearing a bonnet and was afraid her face would freckle. She found the meagre shade of a grove of coconut trees and sat in it, the wind tugging at her hair. Her eyes were drawn out to the ships in the harbor. *Good Bess*, a monster dominating the horizon. And Alexandre's schooner, neat and unassuming. She wondered what he was doing aboard, if Howlett had already asked him to serve tea and lemonade to Orlanda's self-important guests. Tears began to fall. She could deny it no longer. She loved him. She had schooled herself to be practical, rational. But practicality and rationality had melted away. The thought of Alexandre filled her with wild, raw feelings.

Constance pulled her shoes and stockings off and

plunged her feet into the warm sand, closing her eyes. Her jealousy had made her speak harshly to Orlanda, but the tirade was as easily applied to herself. It was hopeless for her to be in love with Alexandre. Utterly hopeless.

And yet, she was still in love with him.

The sounds of the sea rushed around her. She replayed all her encounters with Alexandre in her imagination. His noble, brave silence when he first boarded *Good Bess*. The feel of his hard back pressed against her when he carried her to her mother's house. The rough warmth of his hand . . . The dull ache intensified within her. She began to imagine other encounters, being held close in his arms, the tickle of his hair on her face, his lips at her throat . . .

"Constance!"

She opened her eyes. Father was approaching, the sun glinting on his dark auburn hair. She felt guilty, as though he could see her thoughts. She pulled her toes out of the sand and reached for her shoes.

He stopped, gazing down sternly. "What did you do to Orlanda?"

"Why? What has she said?"

"She has said very little. But she returned to the house a few minutes ago awash in tears. Her father is on business in town, her mother is unwell, and so I have been charged with the task of admonishing you for your 'cruel, cruel words.'" He smiled at her, bemused.

Constance relaxed. "She was being foolish, and I told her so," she said.

Father held out a hand to help her to her feet. "It's about time somebody did, Constance. But could you please apologize? We are the Howletts' guests, and the right thing to do is keep the waters smooth."

They began to walk, side by side in the sunshine. "Father, do you ever get tired of doing the right thing? Do you not sometimes want to do the wrong thing?"

He frowned. "Man should be a rational creature, not a slave to his instincts."

She wanted to say, *What about woman?* But she didn't. Instead, she said, "Orlanda tells me that Mr. Howlett intends to press Alexandre into service as a footman at the dance. Do you not think that is too much to ask of him?"

"It's only a dance. I daresay there will be two dozen tedious people in attendance. They'll eat, drink, manage a few figures, go home and forget they ever came. Alexandre is working his way home with us; he'll do what he is asked, I imagine. Though he seems rather a rough creature and will likely drop a potato in somebody's lap." Father suppressed a smile. "Let's hope it's somebody unpleasant."

Constance managed to smile in return and steeled herself to apologize to Orlanda.

———

As Henry rowed, Howlett clutched the sides of the boat so hard that his knuckles turned white. Henry had been aboard *Good Bess*, making sure that all was well. Howlett had business with Alexandre, so they were paying a visit to the *Queen of Pearls* as well.

"Not comfortable on the water, William?" Henry asked.

Howlett smiled sheepishly. "I'm afraid I never got my sea legs. To be honest, it's one of the reasons I've never returned to England. The journey out was so distressing."

Henry nodded to pretend he understood. Inside, he condemned Howlett as a coward. There had to be something wrong with a man who was afraid of the sea. He pulled the oars, his muscles straining. Ordinarily, he'd have one of his officers or crew row for him. But he wanted a few minutes alone with Howlett to discuss the progress of their investigations. At the villa, there was always somebody lurking around.

"I had a letter back from the shipping registrar this

morning," Henry said. "No record of a ship called the *Monkey King*. Faith's name appears nowhere."

"She was with a man, they say. Do you have any idea who that might have been?"

Henry was jolted by his bluntness. "Of course not. For all I know, it was a white slave trader."

"Hmm, which would explain why there was no record with the registrar."

Henry rowed on through the silky water, not telling Howlett how disappointed he felt. He had been here at Nagakodi for three weeks, and his investigations seemed already to have stalled. Enquiries into who owned the little house on the edge of town revealed that Faith still owned it, but no other name appeared on the documents. The sale happened too long ago to discover who had paid for the dwelling, or from where the money was drawn. The neighbor, when approached by Howlett again, remembered the furniture being sold by debtors two years after she had moved out (at least, that was Howlett's translation of what the neighbor had said; Henry had his doubts that it was entirely accurate). It seemed his wife had disappeared, once again, into thin air.

Howlett spoke of a few other friends who might be able to help and promised to get on with writing letters that afternoon. True to his offer to help Howlett with his business in exchange for helping in his search for Faith, Henry agreed to take some accounts into town for him. Their business was sorted quickly, in time to board the pearler.

Alexandre had seen them approach and waited for them to climb up, offering a hand to Howlett to steady him.

"Thank you, boy," Howlett said.

"You're welcome." Alexandre was half-dressed as usual and Henry wondered, not for the first time, how he hoped to adapt to life back in Europe. And yet, that was where his heart was set on going.

"Alexandre, we both have business with you," Henry said. "For my part, I've had word this morning of a buyer from Colombo. He's coming up in a week to inspect the *Queen of Pearls*. I can't imagine a reason he won't buy it, so do make sure it's tidy, ready for him to sail that day."

"Yes, Captain." Alexandre turned his steady gaze to Howlett.

"Yes. Well." He cleared his throat. "As you may know, we are hosting a dance in two nights. I'd like you to come ashore and act as a footman for the evening."

Alexandre nodded, then said, "What is a footman?"

Henry hid a smile. Howlett blustered. "A footman is

a . . . presentable servant. You'll trim the lamps, wait at dinner, fetch lemonade and tea for the ladies and gentlemen at the dance. Ordinarily you'd wear a fine costume, but there's little chance of finding you a powdered wig in this town. You're about my height, so I'll loan you some decent clothes to wear. Come by at six; we'll dress you and send you down."

"As you wish, sir," Alexandre said, his expression giving nothing away.

As they rowed back to shore, Henry began to think about how much money he would get for the pearler. A tidy sum, most likely, as she was solid and well built, of Indian teak. It would go some way to offsetting the huge financial losses of this journey. Now, when he looked back on the moment he had opened Howlett's letter and discovered that Faith might have been in Ceylon, he couldn't believe his own hastiness. Sailing without cargo or commission, sailing without entertaining a shred of doubt that he would find Faith. He hadn't found her. Days were passing without new clues. Perhaps he would try to find a commission nearby and then, when the pearler was sold, head home.

Empty-handed.

Orlanda forgave Constance quickly and kept her busy. One afternoon Constance tried to meet Alexandre at the beach, but was stopped by Father, minding her that shoes were still expected of English girls even in foreign places. Then, the day before the dance, she returned to her room after writing place cards for Orlanda in the library and saw a sight from her window that made her heart leap.

The sun was setting; the horizon was cloudless.

She hurried to the window and looked down. Alexandre was in his customary spot, his drawing book beside him with its pages flapping in the breeze. She couldn't stop herself from smiling and raced out of the room.

She slowed herself on the stairs as she passed Mrs. Howlett, grey-faced and trembling, being helped up by Chandrika.

Then she raced again, out the front door and around to the beach.

Alexandre saw her approaching, stood and waved. He pointed, excited like a child. "No clouds, Constance!" he called.

She hurried to join him, and they stood shoulder to shoulder as the sun grew huge and orange, its reflection blazing unimpeded in the water. His fingers were less than an inch from her own, and it was as though their hands were magnetized to each other. She had to fight hard to resist. But out here in the open she had to behave appropriately. She knew too well how clear the view to this position was from her bedroom window.

As the sun lowered into the water, she imagined herself with Alexandre, far from the eyes of anyone. And knew that, in such circumstance, she couldn't trust herself. She allowed herself to glance away from the sun, to him. His jaw was strong, his nose long and straight, his lips full and soft, his long dark hair tangled on his collar. He turned and saw her looking at him. She didn't turn her eyes away. Instead, they held each other's gaze. The world seemed to drop away from her feet. She felt she might faint.

Then he glanced away, and everything was back to normal.

"Have you heard?" he said. "I am to be a footman at Orlanda's dance."

"I had heard," she replied. "I think it's terrible."

"You think I will make a bad footman?" he teased.

"No, I think it's terrible that you were even asked. It's . . . not . . ."

"I am not trained for such service," Alexandre said. "And yet, I have few choices. In truth, I do not have high expectations of life. I can be happy with very little, so you must not concern yourself for me." He glanced at her, smiling softly. "But thank you, nonetheless. I do not remember a time when somebody cared what happened to me."

"I care," she said, too fervently, but unable to stop herself. "I care very much."

He didn't speak for a long time. The sun disappeared; streaky clouds began to gather. Then he said, "Do not care too much, Constance. For nothing can come of it."

The words were like cold water on her heart. He was rebuffing her? Had her feelings for him been so obvious? She felt like a fool: as silly and cow-eyed as Orlanda. Wounded pride made her bluster. "I don't know what you mean," she said, her voice mock-cheerful. "But I expect I had better get back for supper. They will be waiting for me."

"Goodnight, Constance," he said, picking up his drawing book.

"Goodnight," she said in what she hoped was a practical tone of voice. Then, not knowing what else to say, she walked away in silence.

Chapter 13

Constance couldn't decide what to wear.

Her three dresses had been freshly laundered, but she had packed them for practicality, not prettiness. Tonight, she wanted to look pretty. Not for all the other guests at the dance, but for Alexandre, who she knew would be there.

Orlanda's clothes were too small, though she had an excess of pretty dresses. Mrs. Howlett's were approaching the right size, though they were matronly and severe. Her bed was covered in a pile of discarded clothes, and she stood in her chemise, chewing the inside of her cheek and wondering what she was going to do.

A knock at the door. She quickly pulled on her robe and went to answer it.

"Father?" she said, surprised to see him. He had something behind his back.

"May I come in?"

She opened the door fully, and he revealed that he was

holding a dress of white muslin, embroidered with beads. "I only remembered this morning," he said.

"Remembered?" She took the dress, admiring its crisp whiteness.

"You had been looking for new clothes. That day at the markets."

Constance recalled running into her father on the track to the beach, lying to him about hankering for a dress. "It's beautiful," she said.

"I am not certain it will fit. But you are the same height as me, and I held it up against myself this morning at the dressmaker's shop." His eyes glittered with laughter. "I may have set the dressmaker's mind to wondering. In any case, Chandrika has said she can make a few quick alterations if necessary."

She pressed the dress against her body. It was perfect. "Thank you most sincerely, Father," she said. "Your kindness, your thoughtfulness . . ."

"Surprise you? That is a shame. However, as it is less than a month since you believed me to be a pirate, I shall accept your thanks with good grace." He nodded once, then turned to leave.

She closed the door, carefully unbuttoned the back of the dress and pulled it on. She fastened as many buttons as she could without help, then went to the mirror. It fitted beautifully. Another, gentler, knock at the door alerted her to Chandrika's arrival.

She let the housemaid in. "It's fine, Chandrika," she said. "It fits almost perfectly."

Chandrika admired the dress, then turned Constance around to finish off her buttons. "I'm glad, but I've come to see you about something else." She took Constance's shoulders and turned her back. "My brother-in-law, Nissanka, is here to see you."

"Nissanka? Then he must have news for me."

"I do not know, Miss Blackchurch. But I have asked him to wait under the pergola in the spice garden to speak with you. The house is very busy. I thought you might appreciate the privacy."

"Thank you, Chandrika. I'll just need to avoid—"

"Orlanda is occupied with dressing. I will go to her now."

Constance took Chandrika's hand and squeezed it gratefully. Then she made her way down the stairs and out to the spice garden. Only an hour now before the guests were due to arrive. The dining table was set, the dancing room was prepared, the weather had stayed clear. Orlanda was excited beyond words, but Constance had never been fond of dances or parties. She was far more excited to hear what Nissanka had to say about Ranumaran.

He sat on the carved seat under the pergola. When he saw her, he stood.

"Nissanka, thank you so much for coming to see me," she said. "Shall we sit down?"

"Yes, miss," he said. The sky was growing soft. They settled together on the seat and, without prompting, he spoke.

"I ask my family, my friends in Ranumaran about your 'hidden temple.' Nobody know. They ask their family, their friends. Finally, somebody know."

Constance flexed forward, her heart picking up its speed. "Go on."

"There is no temple in Ranumaran. 'Hidden temple' is a story."

"You mean, like a legend? A myth?"

He shook his head. "Not one of our stories. One of yours. An Englishman story. There is a cave in Ranumaran. I believe this is your hidden temple. They say an Englishman come every day for years, to the cave. Nobody know what he do. He come, he go again after an hour. The locals say, he must pray. It is Englishman's temple. He say he goes there for faith." Here Nissanka smiled. "Your mother's name?"

"Yes. Faith." Constance's mind tried to make sense of this. Her mother lived in a cave? And who was the Englishman who came to see her? Her captor? Did he bring her food and water?

"I am sorry I have nothing but story to tell you. No fact. But he has not been seen for some years now."

She shook her head. It didn't matter. The important thing was that she had another clue to go on. "This cave, how do I get there?"

Nissanka scratched his head. "As for how you get there from here, I don't know. I go up with an elephant. You could sail. You see Ranumaran just after Sun Peak."

"But once I'm in Ranumaran," she said, hoping she didn't sound impatient, "how do I find the cave?"

He smiled, pulling a folded piece of paper out of his pocket. "You follow my map."

Constance opened the paper, scanned it quickly, then folded it once more. "I am in your debt, Nissanka. This means a lot to me."

"I hope you find your mother."

She returned to the villa with the map tucked up her sleeve for safety. She crossed the entrance hall—swarming now with servants hired for the evening—then headed for the stairs, when she looked up and saw Alexandre.

At first, she almost didn't recognize him. He had been groomed so severely. His hair was tied back with a velvet ribbon; he wore a dark-grey waistcoat, a white cravat, black pants with shining boots to his knees, and over the top an embroidered frock coat in yellow and gold. She stopped, agape. He didn't see her, too busy fiddling with a button on his waistcoat. After a moment, he hurried on his way.

It was strange. As much as she thought he looked unspeakably handsome in his fine clothes, she still preferred him as he ordinarily was. Natural, comfortable, a wildflower rather than one grown in a pot on the sill. She shook her head, telling herself to put an end to these thoughts. He had made it clear he entertained no such thoughts of her.

———

The laughing crowd made its way through the garden in moonlight and towards the dancing room. Brightly burning lanterns hung all about, lighting the room to gold. The colored streamers danced. At Orlanda's begging, Mr. Howlett had paid for a fence to be hastily erected on the sea side of the room to block the breeze. But still the sea air enveloped them, fresh and salty. The clavichord stood in the corner nearest the garden, and chairs and small tables had been arranged all around, creating a large round dance floor in the middle.

Constance followed along last. The dinner had been tiresome. She'd been stuck between Orlanda and a carrot-haired Dutch trader's son named Victor. Victor had become fixated on her, trapping her in long, dull conversations about elephant routes, his strong accent making him hard to understand. Orlanda, for her part, had spoken of nothing but how handsome Alexandre looked, how she was sure he was admiring her dress—in truth, there was very little to admire as it was flimsy and almost see-through—and how her father would certainly approve of him as a son-in-law after seeing him behave so gentleman-like. Their two voices seemed to batter Constance from either side. She watched Alexandre going through the motions of waiting the table, so unschooled in the movements that he seemed almost clumsy, and then decided she could watch him no more.

The dancing room was a welcome change from the oppressive heat indoors, but Constance knew she would probably have to spend the evening fighting off Victor's attentions and Orlanda's silly declarations of love. She took a seat by herself, near the clavichord, and hitched her gloves up over her forearms again. She watched the crowd as they gathered, talking and laughing. Most spoke English, though a pocket of Dutch seamen had formed resolutely apart from the rest on the corner closest to the beach, and the two French guests stood together, gazing forlornly at the party swirling around them.

Mrs. Howlett shuffled out, a sheaf of music under her arm. Orlanda approached, impatient and hopeful all at once, and helped her mother to get comfortable at the clavichord. Mrs. Howlett warmed her fingers on a scale, then played the opening chords of the first minuet. Orlanda, as the host's daughter, took her place as the first dancer, with an elderly Dutch gentleman—rumored to be related to Danish royalty—as her partner. Soon, other couples were joining them for the quadrille. Constance was not surprised when Victor appeared before her, a hopeful glint in his eyes.

"Miss Blackchurch?"

She wanted to moan, "I don't feel like dancing." But she didn't, because that would have been rude. Instead, she offered him her arm and they were off.

The thing about the quadrille was that it took so long. Victor returned to his favorite topic of conversation, and Constance took the opportunity to direct her gaze to the refreshment table. There was Alexandre, standing with his noble back erect, gazing directly at her.

She smiled. He didn't return her smile. In fact, he was almost scowling. Then she was whirled around again, facing the other way for the next figure. When the dance turned again, he was pouring tea for the French couple, talking to them. She had the odd feeling that she had displeased him somehow. She became aware that Victor had stopped speaking and realized she had been asked a question.

"I'm sorry? I didn't hear you properly over the music," she said.

"I said, have you ever ridden an elephant?"

"No," she said.

"You really should experience it while you are here."

Elephants. Nissanka had suggested that was one way to get to Ranumaran. "Where does one go to find an elephant for travel?" she asked.

He began to explain, and for the first time in the evening she was interested in him, as he promised her use of one of his own personal elephants—apparently he had a number of them—should she ever need to take a journey on land. After the dance, they retired to sit, still talking. Victor asked her if she wanted lemonade, then headed to the refreshment table to fetch it.

Alexandre was still looking in her direction, still without a smile on his lips. She suspected he might be jealous. She was both thrilled and saddened by the thought. Thrilled because it meant he did feel something for her, but saddened because she knew that even though Alexandre was much more noble and intelligent than her dancing partner, her father would still rather see her married to Victor. Something was wrong with the world when fathers would rather their daughters were with the right man than with a good man.

The night wore on. Constance only managed to be apart from Victor for brief periods, pleading that she should dance with somebody else or risk idle gossip. Orlanda danced with everybody at least once and flirted outrageously with the ship's officers, her eyes always turned to Alexandre to gauge his reaction. Father's first officer, Maitland, seemed absolutely smitten with Orlanda, though she barely gave him a second glance. Mrs. Howlett began to flag, her fingers fumbling into the cracks between the keys, her tempos speeding and slowing, forcing the dancers to do the same. Alexandre stonily served refreshments, nowhere near as friendly and polished as the native servants in their brightly colored wraps. Father played cards behind the refreshment table while Mr. Howlett smoked cigars and took the occasional turn about the room to supervise. Sometimes, when being whirled about in a dance with other couples, Constance would catch a glimpse of the sky, a breath of the salt air, the sound of the sea in the distance, and it would all seem so strange. An English country dance, on the edge of the beach in a faraway place. It was almost magical. If only her dance partner was Alexandre, and not the tedious Victor.

"I simply can't dance again," Constance said to him, as he urged her to stand up with him once more.

"Well, then we shall have some tea. Come."

Constance eyed the refreshments table. Alexandre in his fine clothes. "I'd rather just sit—"

"No. I insist. You've clung to the corner of the room all evening. Please accompany me. I know my father would like to meet you." He offered his arm, and she could do nothing but take it and approach Alexandre as though she belonged to Victor.

"Two cups of tea, boy," Victor said to Alexandre.

Alexandre, unsmiling, not meeting her eyes, lifted the milk jug and made to pour.

"No, no. The milk doesn't go in first. You'll scald it. Really, boy, where did you learn your manners?" Victor turned to see if Constance was admiring his exercise of authority. She was horrified into silence and didn't know where to look. "Rather a surly fellow, isn't he?" Victor said, as though Alexandre wasn't there to hear it.

Constance finally turned her eyes to Alexandre, whose cheeks had flushed. He wouldn't meet her gaze.

"Hey, fellow," Victor said, leaning on the table with his fists. "Would it hurt you to smile at the lady?"

Constance didn't know if what happened next was an accident. Alexandre was bumped from behind by one of the other servants, his elbow jolted forward, and scalding tea splashed from the spout of the pot over Victor's left wrist and forearm. The next few minutes blurred as Constance watched helplessly. Victor shouted in pain; immediately a dozen people were crowded around them, offering various remedies for burns. Mr. Howlett arrived, barking at Alexandre for his clumsiness. Alexandre shrugged out of the frock coat, handed it over wordlessly and stalked off towards the beach. Howlett, the coat under his arm, dragged Victor up towards the house, promising that Chandrika had a salve that could take the sting out of anything. Constance was afraid she would cry, so she extricated herself from the crowd and ran headlong into Orlanda, who was on the verge of chasing Alexandre down to the beach. Constance seized her, held her still.

"What happened? Where's he going?" Orlanda cried.

Constance explained, and Orlanda's eyes filled with tears. "Oh, Alexandre. Proud, fiery Alexandre! What have you done?" She made little fists with her hands. "Father will be most displeased; Father will never let him anywhere near me again!"

Constance put an arm around her friend's shoulders, thinking exactly the same thing.

Chapter 14

Constance was somewhere in the space between sleep and wakefulness, when she heard a soft sound. Her eyelids fluttered open, and she held her breath a moment in the dark, but didn't hear it again. She remembered the events at the dance that evening, and her heart sank all over again. She turned on her side and closed her eyes, chasing sleep.

The sound again.

This time she rose. It had come from her window, a soft *click*. Another. She opened the window and looked down.

Alexandre stood directly below her window, poised to throw up another shell. His hair caught the moonlight; the sea breeze tugged at his clothes. The sea, oblivious to the quiet sleepiness of the world, was loud and vigorous. He saw her and beckoned silently with both hands. He wanted her to come down.

Constance pinched the delicate skin on the inside of her wrist. No, she wasn't dreaming; this was real. Alexandre *really* waited beneath her window for her. To join him would be entirely scandalous, especially after the incident at the ball, just a few hours ago.

Constance quickly pulled on a dress, leaving her hair unbound and her shoes in the corner of the room. The house was silent, dark. She held the banister as she felt her way down the stairs toe by toe, holding her breath until she shut herself in the library. The French doors squeaked on their hinges softly. She paused, bracing herself. Nobody woke. Nobody came. Heart thundering, she slipped outside.

Alexandre was waiting for her in the dancing room, back in his own clothes. The streamers were sagging and tattered; the chairs and tables had all been stacked into the centre of the room. The smell of cigar smoke had been washed away by the sea air. Constance approached Alexandre, her feet prickling with excitement.

He held out his right hand to her, at the level of his shoulder. Curious, she took it. Without a word, he swung her arm gently and began the steps of the first minuet that had been played that evening. Delighted, she joined him. Their bare feet were silent on the flagstones. Alexandre knew the whole figure, and she wondered if he had learned it merely by watching it that evening. Constance laughed.

No music, no lights, no gloves, no shoes, no complicated hairstyles and fancy clothes. Just the two of them and the sea air, spinning through the dance. His body seemed so close, his warm hands so strong. . . .

The dance came to its end, and he dropped her hand and stood back.

She caught her breath. "When did you learn to do that?"

"When I was a small boy, I knew a woman who was only three feet high. She taught me to dance. All other partners were too tall for her."

She considered him in the dark. "So you are more cultured than Orlanda gave you credit for?"

He scowled. "Why would I care to be cultured, when that boorish Dutch fellow should be considered a shining example of culture? He is a rude pig."

"Is that why you poured hot tea on him?"

The edges of a smile touched his mouth. "That was an accident. Though it pleased me greatly."

A long moment of silence stretched out. Constance reluctantly said, "I should get back."

Alexandre shook his head. "No. Come with me for a walk on the beach. It's a beautiful night."

"Alexandre?"

"Everything will change tomorrow, Constance," he said quickly. "Howlett will poison your father's opinion of me. I will be forced off *La Reine des Perles*, he will withdraw his offer of my passage back to France, and I won't see you again. Say you'll come with me."

Constance's heart caught in her throat. Was he right? Perhaps. And if it were true, if she were never to see him again after tonight, she didn't want to regret forever that she didn't walk with him. She wasn't afraid of the opinions of others; she wasn't even afraid of her father's anger. She was only afraid of losing a secret moment that would never come again.

"I will come with you," she said.

The sand took on a grey-blue sheen in the soft moonlight. They walked in silence a while, leaving the villa behind them around the curve of the headland. In time, only the jungle, the sand and the ocean existed, and they were the last two souls on the edge of the world. Alexandre took her hand in his, and while she was afraid she might faint, she didn't. Every muscle in her body ached with the effort of trying to hang on to this sensation as tightly as she could. Away from the harbor, the ocean roared on, as it had since the world began.

Finally, they came to sit on the warm sand, and

Constance tried to reassure Alexandre that the situation wasn't as dire as he thought.

"Father is a reasonable man," she said. "He'll understand it was an accident."

"It wasn't an accident when I stormed off because Howlett shouted at me."

"French pride," Constance teased.

He smiled at her, then dropped his voice. "I never act like that, Constance. *Never.* I have been shouted at by worse men than William Howlett, and usually I just endure it. Hardship schools you to endure anything. An irate rich man is of little concern to me."

"Then why?" she said.

"Because tonight it mattered. Because you were watching. I didn't want you to think me so low, that . . ." He trailed off.

Tears pricked her eyes. "I do not think you low. You are so noble and so . . ." Words failed her. Her heart hammered with the thrill of love as much as the excitement of being so far outside the rules.

He pulled his knees up to his chest and rested his chin on them. "In truth, I think I was jealous too. Seeing you with that Dutchman, in his arms." He turned to look at her in the soft dark. "Do you think me a fool, Miss

Blackchurch? To have grown to care who a lady well above my station dances with?"

"Not at all, Monsieur Sans-Nom," she said in return.

"The world is very different here, is it not? The English rules don't seem to fit." He ran his hands through his hair, making a noise of exasperation. "There is no hope for me, Constance. You will likely marry a man better bred than me, and there's little we can do about it. But this fact changes nothing. I still feel the way I feel. . . ."

"How do you feel?" she prompted.

He turned his face to her, considering her. His eyes were black, deep as the ocean. "I feel . . . love."

A warm sensation fluttered over her skin. Her mouth moved to speak, but she could not. He leaned forward, resting his palm in the sand. She leaned in to him, slowly. His mouth closed over hers. She let her eyes drift shut. His lips were hot, slightly salty. Her pulse hammered in her ears, and she wondered if it might be possible to die from a kiss. She thought it would be a nice way to go.

In time, he drew back, fixing her gaze in his. "You are so beautiful," he said quietly, the ocean threatening to obliterate his words entirely. "Whatever shall I do without you, Constance?"

Right then, if he had asked her to run away with him,

she would have said yes. She would have said yes to any suggestion, no matter how unreasonable or improper. But he didn't suggest any such thing to her.

Instead, he said, "It is impossible to believe that only a month ago I could get along fine without you, but now the prospect of returning to that way of being is awful to me."

"Is it really so hopeless?" she said, knowing it was a foolish thing to say.

He didn't answer. The sea beat its ceaseless rhythm. Melancholy washed through her. She remembered she hadn't even told him about the map, the cave that Nissanka had spoken of. What was the point? If things went as badly as he thought, then she would have to continue her search without him.

No. She still had some say in the matter. She determined that she would speak to Father first thing in the morning, explain the situation, how Victor had been rude, how the accident had happened, how Howlett had roared at Alexandre so improperly.

Alexandre stood and helped her to her feet. "You should get back," he said. "There's no point in both of us getting in trouble."

She stood facing him, then boldly pressed herself against

him. His arms encircled her, and she could hear his heart thumping in his chest. Then he released her. "Come. The sun will be rising soon."

Constance made it in through the library, up the stairs, and into her room without arousing suspicion. She was drifting on a cloud of euphoria, re-imagining the feel of Alexandre's lips on hers over and over. She closed the door quietly behind her, then turned to see Orlanda lying very still on her bed. Puzzled, she approached, parting the mosquito netting. At first she thought Orlanda asleep, but then she spoke.

"Good morning, Constance." A snaky tone, one she hadn't heard before.

"Orlanda. What are you doing here?"

Orlanda sat up. "I heard you leave."

Constance's heart froze over. What did Orlanda know? She thought about the view of the beach from her own window. What had Orlanda seen?

"Where have you been?" Orlanda asked.

Constance relaxed a little. So she hadn't actually *seen* anything. "I couldn't sleep. I thought a walk on the beach would help me relax," she said.

"Liar!" Orlanda cried, her voice suddenly passionate.

"I saw you. I saw you with . . . him."

"Shh," Constance said desperately. "You'll wake the whole house."

"I saw you standing on the beach, talking to him. And then you went off and . . . Constance, what have you done?"

"Nothing. We talked, that's all. Don't tell my father. Please, Orlanda, as my friend I—"

"Talking and walking? That is all?" Orlanda snorted. "Rubbish. I know boys. I know what they like to do. Why, when we were living in Colombo I did a few unforgivable things myself."

Constance threw her forearm over her head. Orlanda's coy talk about romance cheapened love so. "I'm tired, Orlanda. I need to sleep. Please, forget what you have seen tonight. It was of no consequence."

Orlanda wouldn't let the topic go. "You can pretend all you like that you are a well-behaved English girl," she said. "But I know the truth. And I shant forget anything."

The door closed quietly as Orlanda left.

———

Henry worked at the little writing table in the library. Two shafts of morning sunshine stretched across the rug. He was supposed to be writing letters to creditors for Howlett, but was in fact writing more letters about Faith, the *Monkey King*, the house near the edge of the jungle, the furniture that was sold . . . Letters to English businesses, all along the western coast of Ceylon, in Kandy, in southern India. *Faith Blackchurch*. He had written her name so many times now that it seemed to have lost its meaning. As though she wasn't a real person anymore, but a character in a fairy tale, and just as impossible to find. He realized his tone in the letters was growing increasingly desperate, that it was chipping away at his dignity. The last time he had felt like this— forlorn, robbed of pride—was in the months after she left. Sixteen years later, he was there again. And that was why he had to find her, even if he didn't like what he found. To put these feelings behind him forever.

Constance appeared at the door. Instinctively, he pulled a book over the letter he was writing, blotting all the words. He cursed under his breath. Constance looked puzzled.

"Father?"

"I'm not swearing at you," he said, ashamed to let slip his sailor vocabulary.

She hesitated on the threshold.

"Come in, child. What is it you want?"

She closed the door behind her. "I need to escape Orlanda," she whispered.

"That I can understand. The girl is a chattering fool and would drive most sensible folk away; though Maitland seemed to develop an attachment to her last night." He indicated the bookcase. "Well, pull down the largest volume you can to frighten her off," he said. "You can sit over there, but don't disturb me."

She selected a volume of Chaucer and settled on the sofa with a beam of sunshine on her shoulder. He admired her for a moment: her outward grace as much as her good sense. How it had pained him to see her spend all her time the previous night in the company of that Dutch oaf, Victor Kloppman. But what was he to do? She was a young woman, approaching marriageable age, and there would be plenty of oafs beating a path to her door in the race to win her. Kloppman was a rich, well-bred young man. If she formed an attachment, he would have no grounds to reject her choice. The rules of such arrangements were strict, even when they made no sense. The pit of his stomach tingled with regrets and anxieties. He, of all people, knew how badly such arrangements could turn out. He tried to put these thoughts out of his head and began his letter again. Within minutes, Orlanda was at the door.

"Constance?" she said in an imperious voice.

He adopted his best gruff voice. "Constance is devoting the morning to her studies, which I am much dismayed to find she has neglected so far in her stay."

Constance gave Orlanda a weak smile.

"Oh," Orlanda said, unintimidated. "Perhaps I could sit with you?"

"If you please."

It took seven minutes for her to grow bored, and then she was gone. Quiet returned to the library. Henry worked; Constance read. After a time, he became aware of restless energy in the room. He glanced around to see that Constance had put her book aside and was fidgeting in her seat, eyes turned towards the French doors.

"What is it, Constance?"

She met his gaze. "May I be very honest with you, Father?"

"I should hope that you were only ever honest with me."

She nodded, chose her words, then began to speak. "Something happened at the dance last night. . . ."

Here it was, then. She was about to declare her love for Kloppman. He put his pen aside, trying to force all his muscles to relax. "Yes, child?"

"A wrong was committed, and greater wrongs may proceed from it unless you are a generous and reasonable man."

This was a surprise. "So this isn't about Kloppman?"

"Kloppman?"

"Victor. That young man you danced with all night. I had thought that you might have formed an attachment. . . ."

An expression of impatience and distaste crossed her face. "Good lord, no. No."

"I am glad," he said with real relief. "He seems to me rather too dull-witted for you."

Encouraged, she began to speak very quickly. "He was very rude, Father, especially to Alexandre, who was struggling with the tasks of a footman. Victor and I were getting tea, when another of the servants knocked Alexandre's elbow and hot tea went all over Victor's wrist. It was a genuine accident, and I saw it with my own eyes. Howlett had no right to shout at Alexandre so." Here she paused for breath. He noted that her cheeks had flushed.

"You are very passionate about it."

"I do not like to see an injustice done against an innocent man."

Any pride he felt at her sense of justice was tempered

by his suspicion that more than justice was at stake. "Howlett said Alexandre threw a coat at him and stalked off into the night."

Here she slowed, not meeting his eyes. "I would have done the same, had I been so affronted. I want to ensure that Alexandre is not put off on shore, that he still has his opportunity to return to Europe."

Henry veiled a smile. Of course he had endured Howlett's complaints about Alexandre and his demands that Henry put him off. But Henry hadn't taken him seriously. Howlett had all but invited the situation: letting Alexandre into his home to teach his daughter French, then dressing him up and unleashing him on society when it was clear he hadn't the skills. "Constance, you have spoken very clearly and warmly in defense of the young man. Alexandre and I have something in common, and that is an enemy named Gilbert de Locke. I am unlikely to abandon him here with so little cause. Still, I will go to speak to him today, and I will mind him to stay away from all young ladies and their parties until we sail. Within a week, the pearler will be sold, and he will join the rest of my crew on *Good Bess*. I'll explain to Howlett that, as poor a footman as he is, Alexandre is a valued member of my crew."

She nodded decisively, then picked up her book again. "Thank you, Father."

Unease troubled him. For all her pretense of reason, he could see her hands trembling. How deep did her feelings for the young Frenchman run?

Chapter 15

De Locke waited inside the hot, crowded tavern. Only meagre sunlight struggled through the criss-crossed wooden shutters. The smell of men, beer and mud was overwhelming. He drank his glass of claret, wondering how long past the appointed hour he should stay before he gave up.

The door opened, letting a band of bright sunlight in. Hubert Rachet, the crooked friend of a crooked friend, stood outlined in light for a moment. Then the door closed and he was heading towards de Locke in the dim room.

"Sorry I'm late," he said, reaching for the wine bottle and filling a glass to the brim. "Got held up."

Rachet worked in the offices adjoining the shipping registrar. De Locke's own attempts to find Blackchurch had stalled. *Good Bess* had not come to Colombo, and there was no record of his voyage with the East India Company, so he had paid Rachet to investigate, to see if he could find any information about Blackchurch's whereabouts. Well, he had promised to pay him. Given he'd already sold his pocket watch to buy a pistol, Rachet would be waiting some time for actual money.

"Have you got anything for me?"

"I have." He gulped his wine, splashing it on his cravat. "I don't know what Blackchurch is up to, but it's not trade. He's written two letters to the registrar requesting information about a ship called the *Monkey King* that was rumored to be in these parts sixteen years ago. Left an address at Nagakodi, a port town about a hundred miles north." He pointed straight up, as though towards heaven.

"I know Nagakodi," de Locke said. "A pearl town, though I've never been there."

"That's where your man is." Rachet gulped down the rest of his wine, and de Locke smiled and leaned forward to fill his glass again. The drunker he was, the more likely he was to forget about money.

"I can't thank you enough," de Locke said. "Now, let's talk about finding me a passage to Nagakodi."

———

Alexandre stood on the deck of *La Reine des Perles*, gazing towards the shore. It was sunset, and he was fighting the strong urge to go and sit on the beach, where he knew Constance would see him and join him. But her father had been very clear: stay away.

Two simple words, but so complicated. How could he stay away from Constance, when his whole body was drawn to hers? When he was intoxicated by her? When he knew she still needed him to help find her mother? And yet, stay away he must, or risk Captain Blackchurch leaving him behind here in Ceylon, where the only thing he was good for was pearl diving, and where de Locke would eventually find him.

He became aware of motion on the shore, near the Howletts' villa. A figure, struggling with Howlett's rowboat, trying to get it into the water. It was a woman, and at first he thought it was Constance and his heart picked up its speed. But then she turned her face up, and he saw it was Orlanda.

Orlanda couldn't row a boat.

He leaned on the railing, watching in amusement. Her skirts were dragging in the water as she tried, most inelegantly, to climb into the boat. Finally, she fell forwards into it. She managed to get herself upright and pulled on the oars. Went around in circles for a few moments. He knew she was coming to see him, and he also knew she'd never make it so he wasn't worried about what nonsense she had in mind. He went inside and rummaged in the cupboard for cheese and bread, ate his meal, and returned to the deck.

She was still there, about a hundred feet off shore now. Was that the sound of her wailing? She had given up, the oars were tucked in, and she was drifting forlornly, crying her heart out.

Alexandre sighed. Now he would have to go and get her.

He climbed down into his boat, untied it and began to row. The sun had slipped away, and the water was dark. She would be frightened, possibly cold . . . but he couldn't find any sympathy in his heart for her.

She saw him coming and began to wave madly. He adopted a grim expression and pulled up next to her.

"You came for me!" she sighed. "Oh, I thought I was done for! I thought I would drown!"

He tied her boat to his wordlessly and began to row towards shore.

"Not speaking to me, Alexandre? Has my father forbidden it? Oh, cruel Father! How am I to learn French without you? How am I to go on?"

As he rowed, she kept talking. And talking. Finally, he helped her ashore. She tripped—rather too extravagantly to be genuine—and fell into him. He caught her and tried to stand her back up. But she clung to him like a limpet.

"Alexandre," she said. "They have forbidden us to be together, but my parents know little about what I do. Meet me on the path to town, tomorrow at dawn."

He extricated himself from her embrace, putting his hands in front of him, palms out, to keep her away. Finally, he spoke. "No, Orlanda."

"You needn't worry. I'll be careful that Father doesn't find out."

"No. Orlanda, no."

"But I love you! Love is more important than rules, than the opinions of others."

It is, he thought. "I don't love you, Orlanda."

"Come now," she said, laughing nervously. "Of course you do. I've seen it in your eyes. Your feelings for me—"

"Are not love. You are a nice girl, but I do not love you. I could never love you." He pushed his boat back into the water and climbed in. "Please, stay out of boats. I shouldn't like you to come to any harm."

She began to cry, great howling sobs.

He rowed, until the sound of the sea drowned her out.

Constance paced her room. It was nighttime and she was supposed to be sleeping, just as everybody else in the villa was sleeping, but she couldn't rest.

She needed to speak to Alexandre. She had gone over this in her head a hundred times. To get to Ranumaran alone was impossible. She could ask Victor for help with his elephants, but it would require too much intimacy. Already, she had fended off three of his calling cards. She couldn't walk that far through jungles and swamps, and she certainly couldn't row. But the *Queen of Pearls* would make the journey in just a few hours, and it was her father's ship after all. . . .

But how to speak to Alexandre? He had stopped coming to the beach at sunset, no doubt warned away by Father. Days were slipping by, and Ranumaran seemed to be getting further and further away.

She went to the window. The beat of the ocean. A piece of moon. Was he looking towards shore, thinking of her too? Her face flushed as she remembered the last time they had seen each other.

This was the other pressing reason to see Alexandre: because she simply *had to*. Because if she didn't she would wither and die, like a flower denied sunlight.

Constance moved to the dresser and grabbed her

rushlight in its pretty tin lamp. She placed it in the window. If he were looking, he might see the light; he might deduce she needed to see him. She kept her dress on, refusing to admit the possibility that he wouldn't come, and lay down to wait.

Within half an hour, the rattle came. A shell, hitting the lamp. She rose and went to the window. There he was. She waved, then indicated he should meet her at the dancing room.

Silently, silently through the house, clutching Nissanka's map in her hand. Then running through the garden and into his arms.

He kissed her. The world slowed down a few moments, then he stood back. His eyes were dark pools. "I'm glad you called me," he said.

"I'm glad you came."

"I shouldn't be here."

"I know. But I need your help." She handed him the map and urged him out onto the moonlit beach. He examined it closely as she explained what Nissanka had told her.

"I need to get to Ranumaran," she said. "And the only way I can think of to get there is by sea."

"On *La Reine des Perles*," he said, nodding. "But

Constance, I can't sail her single-handedly. You'll have to help."

"I'll do whatever I have to," she said. "I'm so grateful."

"We'll have to sail at night," he said. "Your father will notice the pearler is missing otherwise."

Constance felt a pang of guilt, realizing suddenly that Alexandre had much more to lose than she did. If they were discovered, Father would not give him another chance.

Alexandre seemed to read her thoughts. "It's all right, Constance. He won't find out. With good winds we'll be there and back before dawn."

"And if he does find out," Constance said, "I'll tell him I ordered you. It's his ship, after all, and I'm his daughter and . . . by then we'll have found Mother so he'll be too busy thinking about that." She took a deep breath, trying to convince herself that it was all true.

Alexandre grasped her hands, bringing them to his lips. "I'd do anything for you," he murmured, his hot breath tickling her fingers.

A gorgeous, melting feeling coursed through her.

"You should go." He released her. "Sleep, Constance. Sleep as much as you can, for there will be none tomorrow night. Meet me here at midnight."

"I will."

Alexandre was in his hammock, sleeping late into the morning, when he heard voices up on deck. He pulled on a shirt and climbed up, to see Captain Blackchurch, Howlett, and a man he thought might be the captain's first officer Maitland, boarding *La Reine des Perles*. Finally, being helped up by her father, was Orlanda. Alexandre straightened his back, puzzled and a little worried. Had something happened to Constance? Had they discovered his plans to sail away that night?

The sun shone on Orlanda's fair hair, illuminating it to white. She pouted, blazing anger in her eyes. "Search his cabin," she said. "For I am sure you'll find it there."

"What is happening?" Alexandre asked.

Captain Blackchurch and Howlett exchanged glances. Finally, Blackchurch spoke in a weary tone. "Alexandre, you are accused of the theft of an item of Orlanda's jewelery."

"It's a golden bird on a chain," she said. "Do you deny you have it?"

Alexandre was momentarily baffled, then he remembered the necklace she had given him. Heat rushed over him as he realized how much trouble he was in. He couldn't speak, and Howlett took his silence for guilt.

"You were in my daughter's room, were you? Amongst her things?" Howlett jabbed him with a finger. "After all I've done for you."

Done for him? Alexandre didn't point out that Howlett had done nothing for him, that Captain Blackchurch's kindness and generosity were things to be treasured but that Howlett had treated him at best off-handedly, at worst, contemptuously.

He found his voice. "I don't deny that I have the item; you will find it hanging on a nail in my cabin," he said. "But I did not steal it. Orlanda gave it to me willingly, despite my protests."

"Lies!" Orlanda cried.

Alexandre had always thought her pretty, but today he saw that she was not. She had a nasty little face, rather like a parrot.

"It is not a lie," he said.

"Go ahead and search," Blackchurch said to Maitland, who disappeared below.

Howlett scowled at Alexandre. "Why would Orlanda give *you* such an item of value willingly?"

"Ask her yourself. For my part, she declared love for me just yesterday morning."

"More lies!" Orlanda shrieked.

"Nonsense!" Howlett cried. "I have raised my daughter well enough, lad, that she knows the difference between a good man and a bad one."

Maitland emerged, holding the glistening chain in one hand. He offered it to Orlanda, eyes soft with barely disguised adoration. "I found it, Miss Howlett."

She snatched it from his fingers.

Howlett turned to the captain. "Blackchurch?"

Captain Blackchurch pondered a moment. A gull swooped overhead, cawing.

How Alexandre wished he could grow wings and fly away with her.

"Alexandre, this is a grave thing you are accused of. Have you any proof that you didn't steal the necklace?"

"I have no proof, sir, only my word."

"I'm sorry, then, lad. Pack your things, we'll take you ashore. Maitland, you stay here and mind the pearler."

"I'll have you in prison for this," Orlanda said triumphantly.

"Nobody's going to prison," Blackchurch said harshly, making Orlanda jump. "You have your necklace returned to you. Alexandre has lost his place in my crew. That evens the situation."

Alexandre swallowed his rage, as years of practice had taught him to. As he gathered together his few possessions, it wasn't his own predicament he was thinking of, but Constance's. How would she get to Ranumaran without him?

Chapter 16

Constance sat on the beach. It was already past midnight, but she kept herself from examining that fact too closely. He would be here, of course he would. Why, he was probably right at this moment on the water in his little rowboat, having overslept. Or had gone back to get something.

She yawned, lying back on the sand. The rushlight she had brought with her glowed eerily in the dark. The moon was behind clouds tonight. Alexandre would be disappointed. He had been relying on moonlight to help them find their way. Still, the cloud might move on. She cheered herself. If Alexandre ever got here. He really was very late.

Time passed. The clouds parted, moved, reformed. The sea beat on, marking the minutes. Constance sat up, straining her eyes to see any sign of Alexandre. What was she to do? If she went home, and he came late . . . But she couldn't wait here all night. She grew anxious. What if he was hurt? Sick? The Howletts had a boat. Should she find it, row out to *La Reine des Perles*? She wasn't a bad rower; her father had taught her on the river when she was little, and her size made her strong.

But what if Alexandre was constrained for some other reason? Perhaps Father had discovered their plan somehow and was lying in wait on the pearler to prove his suspicions?

Constance rose and began to pace. Indecision twisted her up. *Something* had happened, of that she was sure. Alexandre would not idly break his word. But she had no idea what that *something* was, and it made her angry not to know.

Finally, when she was certain that it must have been at least three in the morning, she decided to go home. Her disappointment was keen. She had hoped by now to be well on the way to the hidden temple of Ranumaran, to finding her mother; an adventure to be shared with Alexandre.

Alexandre. What if he had simply changed his mind? What if he had decided he didn't love her, that she wasn't worth the trouble? The ground dissolved beneath her; her heart ached. If only she didn't love him so hard. . . .

Back in her room, she placed the rushlight in the

window and went to bed. Still, in hope, dressed. Sleep caught her, morning came, and Alexandre didn't.

—◦—

Shortly before noon, Constance left the house to go down to the beach again. Just to gaze at Alexandre's schooner and hope that he would read her mind and come to her with explanations. As she passed the spice garden, she thought she heard somebody weeping. Alarmed, she let herself into the garden and found Orlanda, sitting beneath a cinnamon tree, crying into her sleeve.

"Orlanda? Is all well with you?"

Orlanda forced a smile. "Yes, quite, quite well." Then she liquefied into sobs again, and Constance went to sit with her in the shade and put an arm around her.

"There, there," she said. "What has happened to you to make you so upset?"

"Nothing has happened to me." She sniffed, wiped her face on her sleeve, and met Constance's eyes. "What does guilt feel like, Constance?"

"Do you not know?"

"I . . . I don't think I've ever felt it before now. Is it like a sick sadness, very low in one's belly?"

"What did you do?" Constance's skin prickled; she had the awful suspicion that she drew close now to the reason that Alexandre had failed to appear last night.

Orlanda seemed to be searching for words, her little mouth opening and closing like a fish drowning in air.

"Orlanda, what did you do?" Constance said more forcefully.

"I love Alexandre," she said, screwing her hands into fists and beating her chest with them. "I love him until it hurts me. But he rebuffed me, he was so . . . he said he could never love me and it was like scales had been taken from my eyes and I saw . . . that he . . ." She took a deep breath, getting her thoughts in order. "I rather think you have his heart, Constance."

"And this is why you are crying? What was all the talk of guilt?"

"I was angry, I wanted to hurt him for saying I was so unlovable." She wouldn't meet Constance's eyes. "I accused him . . . falsely . . ." Haltingly she described the whole situation, while Constance grew more and more frantic. Alexandre without a job, without a passage home, without a place to live. Constance without a way to find her mother, and all because of Orlanda.

Constance rose to her feet. "Orlanda, you have done a terrible wrong, and you must make it right."

"What can I do?"

"You can go and tell my father and yours that you lied."

"Oh, no. I'll be in ever so much trouble. Father will be so disappointed to see I've been telling lies about boys again."

"Again?" Constance's veins seemed to shake with angry injustice.

"In Colombo. I told you about the boy who tried to climb into my bedroom?" She at least had the decency to blush. "I invited him. It all came out much later, after we'd left town.

"If Father thought that I'd gotten myself in more boy trouble, he would be so angry, he would take away every one of my joys." She shrugged. "Alexandre had nothing, so nothing is easy for him to endure again. But I am not schooled for deprivation. I can't tell Father."

"Then I shall."

Anger blazed in Orlanda's eyes. She climbed to her feet and set her chin defiantly. "And I shall deny everything."

A million words leapt to Constance's lips, none of them complimentary. She swallowed them, turning wordlessly and stalking away.

"Constance? Please?" Orlanda whined. "Don't be

angry with me. I don't have any other friends!" Orlanda sobbed and wailed, but Constance didn't turn back.

She tried to get her emotions under control before entering the library. It wouldn't do to go to Father too impassioned. She knew he already suspected that she had special feelings for Alexandre. She took deep breaths, paced eleven times outside his door, then knocked lightly.

"Come in." Howlett's voice. She was unprepared for that. Her composure had begun to disintegrate before she'd even opened the door.

Howlett sat on the sofa; Father stood with his back to the bookcase. They had been discussing something important, she could tell. They were both tense. Her knees began to tremble, and tears pricked her eyes.

"Father," she said, "I need to speak with you on a most urgent matter, in confidence." She didn't meet Howlett's eyes.

"Now, Constance?"

She wavered. Good sense told her to wait, to come back when she was more composed. But before she could agree to return later, Father had asked Howlett if he'd mind leaving them a few minutes. Howlett agreed, closing the door to the library behind him.

Father turned to her with a steady gaze. "What is it, child? You look quite pale."

"A terrible injustice—" she began.

"Another injustice?" he said quickly. "Concerning Alexandre, I presume?"

She nodded, all the while feeling that the situation was slipping beyond her control. She took a deep breath. "Just now, in the garden, Orlanda confessed to me that she had given Alexandre the necklace. Had, in fact, forced it upon him with declarations of . . . love. When he rebuffed her, she took her revenge by accusing him of theft. Now she has said she will deny the whole story, but she told me and it is the truth."

"I've no doubt it's the truth, Constance. I am forty-two years old. I am a good judge of character. Orlanda is much more likely to concoct a story than Alexandre is to steal jewelery."

It was as though clouds had parted, letting in sunlight. Constance cheered up. "Then you'll reinstate Alexandre? All will be as it was?"

Father shook his head. "I cannot do that."

Despair again. "Why not?"

"Because it would show Howlett that I doubted his judgment, that I thought his daughter a boy-mad liar."

"But what do their opinions matter when Alexandre's life and happiness are at stake?"

He shook his head, pacing away from her. "Constance, at least try to hide your passions. I am quite uncomfortable for you."

Tears overflowed and began to run down her cheeks. She palmed them away.

"Alexandre will be fine," Father continued. "He is strong and resourceful and, I dare say, a good deal more intelligent than Howlett has given him credit for. He will find another ship to make his way home on, and he has a pearl he can sell to help him with his new life."

The pearl! How could she have forgotten? She had it, and Alexandre would need it. But he'd never dare to come near the villa to find her now.

And she could explain none of this to Father.

"Where do you think he's gone?" she asked carefully.

Father turned and narrowed his eyes, his mouth turning down at the corners. "If he has any good sense, he'll make his way to Colombo and put as much distance between himself and Miss Howlett as is practical. You would do well to forget about him, Constance. For there was never anything that could come of it."

She felt transparent and flushed with shame. So Father

knew she loved Alexandre. Could he also tell that her relationship with him had been so intimate? Of course not, but at that moment she was as embarrassed as she would have been were she wearing just her underwear.

"Is that all?" he said gruffly.

Wild emotions made her want to say too much. To defend Alexandre more fiercely, to tell Father about the hidden temple, to somehow make her midnight plans come to fruition, even though she knew it was impossible. She held her tongue. "Yes, Father, that is all," she replied.

He sighed, turning away from her again. "My business here has gone badly, child," he said softly, and she was reminded that Father had his own disappointments to deal with. "I am preparing myself to return to England in the very near future. I have a buyer coming for the pearler in a few days, and once that transaction is finalized, there is nothing to detain me here. You should prepare yourself, too. When you are home in England, I imagine this adventure will grow small behind you. Take comfort in that."

The thought made her feel like screaming. *You don't know my heart! I can't forget him; I will never forget him!* She bit her lip, steeling herself. Father was wrong:

Alexandre wasn't on the way to Colombo. He needed his pearl. He would be somewhere close by.

She just had to find him.

On the first day, it rained, so she stayed home. On the second and third days, she walked the muddy tracks into the village—alone because Orlanda was not speaking to her—and asked around at the markets. Too few of the locals spoke English, though many of them spoke Dutch, of which Constance had the barest grasp. It was almost impossible and, even when she could make herself known, nobody had any information about Alexandre.

On the fourth day, in despair of another day having half-conversations with local traders, she took an afternoon walk on the beach, aching to see him sitting in his regular spot, drawing. Of course he wasn't there, so she headed up the beach, letting her tears fall, her ribs crushed under the weight of her disappointment.

She tried to remember the exact place on the sand where he had first kissed her, but couldn't. It had been dark, mysterious, intoxicating. Now the beach glared under the sun, and every grain of sand looked the same as the next. She turned and faced the sea. The huge waves crashed in, a mist of spray hovering around them. The water stretched away forever, azure with an undercurrent of gold, laced with pristine white caps. Home was out there somewhere, miles and miles away. Cloudy skies and damp green grass. She did miss it: it was the landscape of her soul. But the thought of returning there without Alexandre, perhaps without ever seeing him again, made her sad beyond measure.

"Constance!"

She whirled around. At the edge of the beach, beyond the coconut palms and in the shade of the wild vegetation, Alexandre stood, waving his arms. It was like a dream, and she took a moment to understand that it was real.

Then she began to run.

In moments, she was in his arms, kissing him feverishly. He pressed her close, then pulled away, putting her at arm's length. "Are you sure nobody followed you here?"

"I'm sure. Orlanda and I aren't speaking. Father thinks you've gone to Colombo. He doesn't know I still have your pearl." She kicked the ground. "I should have brought it for you. I'm sorry."

"Don't worry. I will get it from you at another time."

Her fingers touched his face. He looked tired. "Where are you sleeping? Are you hungry? Cold?"

"I've set up a little camp, a hundred feet into the jungle. It's not cold, but my food has nearly run out." He grasped her fingers and squeezed them lightly. "But you must believe me when I tell you I have suffered much greater hardship, and you need not worry for me."

"Oh, Alexandre. I'm so sorry. Father knows you are innocent. He cares more about Howlett's opinion than justice, though."

"I suspected as much. It's easier to be rude to a pearl diver than a pearl trader." He smiled, a weary expression. "Though the second cannot exist without the first."

She sighed, leaning into him, listening to his heart beating through his warm chest. "It's so unfair."

"Life is unfair." He stroked her hair. "But what of you? How will you find your mother?"

"I don't know." She stood back, gazing at him. His hair was loose, tickling his cheek softly.

"You could ask the Dutchman to take you there by elephant," he teased.

"I should die if I had to spend two minutes together in his company," she groaned.

Alexandre's eyes went beyond her, to the water. "I've been watching the tides these last few days," he said. "Good sailing weather every morning an hour after dawn. Then the tide dips, and contrary winds blow in the afternoon."

Constance turned to look at the sea. *Good Bess* and *La Reine des Perles* among the other ships in the curve of the harbor. "What are you thinking, Alexandre?" she said, though she suspected she knew.

"If you and I can get aboard the schooner at dawn, we can sail away to Ranumaran, and nobody can follow us. I can still take you, Constance. I have nothing left to lose."

"And I should lose it all for a chance to find my mother," she said under her breath, the sea breeze carrying her words away.

"There is one problem. First Officer Maitland is aboard my vessel. I cannot think of a way to get him off it. I have turned my mind to it again and again, but all my solutions are foolish or risky."

Constance concentrated on the problem. Maitland was Father's most trusted crewman. Alexandre was right: it would be all but impossible to remove him from his post.

Unless . . . A light flickered to life within her. Maitland at the dance, making eyes at Orlanda. Father's grumbled complaint that Maitland had developed an attachment to her.

"We lure him off," she said with a click of her fingers. "With something he wants very badly." She turned her eyes to Alexandre. "Meet me here again tomorrow, in the morning. I will bring you some breakfast, and I will bring pen and ink and paper. We have love letters to write."

Why didn't anybody speak French? De Locke was tired of it. Tired of getting by in English or Dutch, tired of the puttering local language. If only Alexandre were with him . . . but, of course, if the traitorous wretch had been with him, there would be no need for this journey. He simply wanted to be understood. A passage to Nagakodi, with payment due on his return—when, presumably, Alexandre will have been dispatched and the stolen pearl returned to de Locke's possession—was all he required. But in amongst his lack of ready cash and a bewildering array of local customs and holy days, the best he had managed was a passage to Puttalam, with a vague promise that a friend of somebody's brother's friend had a fish-trading business that would take him up and down the north coast once or twice a week.

And so he found himself on a microscopically slow vessel, surrounded by empty baskets that reeked of fish. It was skippered by a prosperous Sinhalese man whose name was unpronounceable, and it wasn't equipped for passengers, so de Locke seated himself on an upturned basket, gritted his teeth, and prepared to wait out the torturous journey.

A number of hours out of the harbor—de Locke had lost count in glaze-eyed boredom—the skipper of the vessel brought him a wooden plate with a hunk of steamed fish on it. "Dinner," he said in heavily accented English.

"Thank you," de Locke muttered, his stomach turning over in revulsion at the spongy flesh, swimming in its own juices. "How long do you think before we are in Nagakodi?"

The skipper shook his head. "No Nagakodi."

De Locke felt a hot shock of alarm. "No Nagakodi? What do you mean, no Nagakodi?"

The skipper looked puzzled. "I tell you back in Puttalam. I go north. I anchor twenty miles from Nagakodi."

De Locke reeled. He remembered the conversation now, but he had misunderstood. He had thought they were *already* twenty miles from Nagakodi. Not that he was going to be put ashore that far from his goal.

"I . . . but . . ." he sputtered, wanting to demand the vessel turn back but realizing the skipper would never agree. "How do I get from there to Nagakodi?"

"Elephant tracks. A day's walk."

A day's walk. He said it as though it were a stroll in a well-maintained garden, rather than fighting his way through jungle.

"And how long before we anchor?"

"Tonight some time." He smiled broadly, revealing gleaming white teeth. "Then you pay me."

"Yes, yes," de Locke muttered. So be it: a twenty-mile hike along an elephant track through the jungle. It would all be worth it to take his revenge. "What is the name of the town where we anchor?"

"Not town. Just village. Very little, but good fishing." The skipper swiped a mosquito on his neck and examined the bloody smear on his palm. "It called Ranumaran."

Chapter 17

Alexandre waited in the morning cool, in the shade of trees, eyes fixed on the beach, watching for Constance. Every particle of him was poised, waiting. Nothing beyond her arrival mattered. Not the fact that he had lost his passage home, nor that he would likely earn more recriminations in running off with Constance on the schooner, nor that she and he could never actually be together once this adventure was over. The moment was all that counted.

She rounded the headland in the distance, a graceful white figure. He had endured so much in his short life, but nothing had ever affected him like being in love. A revolution of his senses. It was as though prior to her arrival he had only been an ignorant boy. Now he was a man, flesh and blood. He stood and lifted his hand. She did the same in return, then began to hurry, as drawn to him as he was to her. A small part of himself, standing outside the tumult of feelings, coolly reminded him that they had both succumbed to extreme folly. She would soon return to England. What then?

What then?

Then she was in his arms, laughing, her sweet-smelling hair touching his cheek, and the question evaporated.

"I have such a store of things in this bag," she said, patting a gunnysack slung over her shoulder. "Would you like to see?"

"Come back to my camp," he said. "Away from the sun." He took her hand and led her into the cool shade of the trees. All he had were his drawing books, a bag with a few clothes in it, and a blanket that Captain Blackchurch had urged him to take. It was spread over the tangled grass. He sat and invited Constance to do the same. As the trees moved in the breeze, the occasional shot of sunlight would pierce through to the ground. The sea roared on, thunderously loud compared with the gentler waves of the harbor. She gave him food: bread and dripping, salt beef, sweet biscuits left over from yesterday's afternoon tea. He tried as hard as he could to eat slowly, civilly, but suspected that he wolfed it down like the starving man he was. She tried to offer him his pearl, but he refused it.

"I have no way of keeping it safe at the moment,"

he said. "Give it to me after we've been to Ranumaran, when I'm ready to barter it for a passage home."

She tucked it away in the sack again, wrapped in fine paper and enclosed in a little wooden box. Then she withdrew from the sack a sheaf of writing paper, a quill pen and a bottle of ink. Ever practical, she arranged the items on the blanket between them.

"I will write a note to First Officer Maitland," she said. "I will sign it from Orlanda, professing her undying love and so on. And you shall write a letter to Orlanda from you, with similar sentiments. Each letter will give instructions to meet at dawn in the dancing room. While Maitland is thus engaged, we will slip aboard the schooner and weigh anchor. Even if he sees us leave and tells Father immediately, he'll never get *Good Bess* ready to sail in time to take advantage of the favorable tide." She nodded. "A neat plan, isn't it?"

He felt his cheeks burning with shame. "Only I can't write well, Constance," he said quickly. "I never learned. I can read. I can draw. I have taught myself letters but never have a chance to practice."

Constance smiled kindly. "Then I will write them both. But you must help me." She uncorked the ink bottle and pulled the first sheet of paper into her lap. "Oh, dear," she said, as the nib left an inky stain. "I need a better surface to write on."

"Use my back," he said, turning it to her and pulling his knees up against his chest.

He heard her arranging herself, then felt her leaning on him. "That's better," she said. "Now, how does this sound? *My dear Mr. Maitland.* Lord, I don't even know Maitland's first name, do you?"

"I do not know."

"It doesn't matter. *Ever since our all-too-brief encounter at the dance, I have thought of nothing but your . . .* What color are his eyes?"

"Blue?"

"*I have thought of nothing but your smiling eyes.* There. That sounds like Orlanda." She dipped her pen. "*Would you meet me at dawn tomorrow, in the dancing room, so that I may look upon your dear countenance once again? Yours, Orlanda.*"

She picked up the paper and blew on the words, then put it aside. "Now, your turn. You tell me what to write. Only I'll have to disguise my hand so she thinks it's yours."

"Orlanda knows I have neither ink nor paper," he said. "Take a page from my drawing book and use the charcoal. It will be messy, but at least she will believe it's mine."

"Good thinking," Constance said, leaning on his back again with a piece of drawing paper. "Go on."

He closed his eyes. The proximity of her body to his was maddening. He forced himself to translate impulses into words and cleared his throat. "*My dearest beloved*," he ventured, and felt the charcoal stick moving. "*Since we met, I have not experienced a thought that didn't turn to you, a dream that wasn't about you. The sight of you makes my body come to life, makes my skin burn and my veins thunder, and I feel madly alive, madly . . .*" He realized she was no longer writing and glanced over his shoulder. "Constance?"

"You're going too fast," she said huskily.

He locked his fingers together and took a deep breath. "I'm sorry. I will keep it simple. *Dear Orlanda, your absence has made me realize my true feelings. Meet me at dawn in the dancing room so I can show them to you.* That will do, and it's almost true."

Constance laughed, scribbling the note, then putting it aside and packing up her things. She turned her dark eyes to him and tilted her head to one side. "Those things you said . . . ?" she started.

"Yes," he answered. "Yes, that is how I feel about you."

She lifted her gaze to the dark canopy above them, and he saw her eyes glistening with unshed tears. "Why must I have been born into such a stupid world, where love must wait upon propriety? It seems that love should bow to no custom but its own."

He grasped her fingers.

"Alexandre, we could run away," she said, all in one breath, as though even saying it terrified her. "We'll have the pearler; I have some jewelery—bits and pieces we could sell."

The fantasy was compelling. Love and endless youth and the sunlit sea. He could almost taste the salty freedom on his lips. He would have to give up very little to achieve such a dream. But she would have to give up everything. Family, security, honor. He loved her enough to refuse her. "You know it's not possible," he said gently.

"Anything is possible, surely." But already she had backed away from the fantasy, her voice uncertain.

"We have only a day left, Constance. From dawn tomorrow until dusk." He smiled. "Twilight to twilight. If that is all that fate can grant us, we should hold on to it tightly and wring every last drop of joy from it."

She sank into his arms, her voice muffled against his chest. "Curse you for being right, Monsieur Sans-Nom."

"Curse you for making me love you, Miss Blackchurch."

Constance's arms ached as she rowed towards the pearler. Already she had delivered Alexandre's letter, folded but not sealed, to Orlanda.

"I found this on the front step," she lied, handing it to her.

Orlanda had frowned and opened it. Then flushed and pressed it against her chest. No longer friends with Constance, she had flounced off wordlessly. Which Constance imagined had been quite an effort.

Now, there was only the letter to Maitland to deliver. As she rowed, she thought about this morning, writing the letters with Alexandre. The firm muscles of his back. Had she really suggested that they run away together? It was the least sensible thing she had ever done. What if he had said yes? The answer to that question frightened her. In this moment, her love for Alexandre was brighter than any star in the galaxy. If he had said yes, why, she would have run away with him. It was that simple.

But not simple. Father would have come after her, just as he had come looking for her mother.

Constance caught her breath. *Her mother*. Was it possible? For the first time in her life, Constance realized that perhaps her mother hadn't been snatched away from her home. Perhaps she had left willingly.

No, that couldn't be. She'd had a beautiful home, a loving husband, a tiny baby. Constance's heart hurt at the thought of that baby—herself—being left motherless so young. No mother would do that, least of all the serenely beautiful Faith Blackchurch.

Constance realized she had stopped rowing. She picked up the oars again. In a few minutes, she was floating next to *La Reine des Perles*, calling out for Maitland.

He appeared on deck, his big square head and thick neck cocked curiously. "Miss Blackchurch?"

"You mustn't tell Father I've been," she said.

"I can promise you nothing," he replied, puffing up with moral dignity. "Captain Blackchurch is my employer."

She dropped an oar and held up the note. "I have a letter for you, from Orlanda."

He was speechless for a few seconds. Then his voice became soft. "Orlanda has sent me a note?"

Constance felt a pang of pity for him. It was one thing

to manipulate Orlanda; she had lied about Alexandre and brought about this situation. But Maitland was innocent. And, it appeared, smitten with Orlanda.

He was already climbing down the rope ladder, leaning out to take the note from her fingers. "I'm honored that she should condescend to write to me. Will you pass on my thanks?"

Constance picked up the oars again and started to turn herself around in the water. "Tell her yourself," she said with a smile. "I'm sure she will be glad to hear it."

Then she was off again. Maitland and Orlanda weren't the only two people with a dawn rendezvous to prepare for.

The early morning was soft. Pale pink clouds streaked the sky as Orlanda let herself quietly out of the library and made her way through the garden. Her heart hammered. Alexandre would be waiting. She had risen an hour ago, spent an age crimping her hair, and tried on six different pair of gloves to match her dress. She wanted to look perfect for him. It was so like noble, beautiful Alexandre to forgive her for what she had done. She longed to repay him in kisses.

Orlanda smiled to herself. She was no stranger to what

young men wanted from young women. The thrill of the idea pressed her heart. How she loved being out here in the dawn light on a secret assignation.

She arrived at the dancing room and saw him standing with his back to her.

But no. That wasn't Alexandre.

He turned and smiled. It was Captain Blackchurch's first officer, Francis Maitland. A nice enough fellow, to be sure, but not her dream-eyed beloved. She froze. He hurried towards her, hands outstretched.

"My darling Orlanda," he said. "I am not good with words, so let me say to you what I have been rehearsing all night in my mind."

Darling Orlanda? What was going on?

He took her hand and pressed it against his heart. "You are the most beautiful woman I have ever known."

"I am?" A little glow inside her.

"All others around you seem pale and serious. Your laugh is like a bell. I love to listen to your sweet voice."

"You do?"

"Oh, yes. Your delightful chatter fills me with joy."

Orlanda became dimly aware that Alexandre *wasn't* coming, that somehow, somebody—Constance, of course!—was playing a trick on her. But she found she didn't mind so much as long as Francis Maitland was enumerating her virtues.

"I have been able to think of little else but you since the dance," he continued. "Your eyes, your smile. Would you be so kind as to turn those eyes, that smile, towards me? It would make me the happiest man in the world."

The secret thrill was back. She offered him her arm. "Come, Francis," she said with a smile. "Let's find a secluded place where we can talk more freely."

<hr />

Constance worked quickly, scribbling a final note for her adventure. This time, it was addressed to her father.

She had woken in the middle of the night, excitement keeping sleep at bay. And in those long hours as she waited for the dawn to come—gathering a change of clothes, sewing Alexandre's pearl into the hem of her skirt for safekeeping, tying up the two bread rolls she had smuggled out of the dining room in a cloth—she had realized that Father would notice her missing at some point that day. That he would worry. If they knew the pearler was gone, they would suspect Alexandre. And Father would jump to the conclusion that they had run away together. Her mother had disappeared without explanation; Constance was determined she wouldn't do the same.

She blotted it, folded it, and placed it under her pillow. If they were searching for her, they would find it. He would read it. He would be impossibly angry, but at least he wouldn't fear the worst.

Constance peered at herself in the looking glass in the dim morning light. Today, her mother might see her for the first time in sixteen years. What would she think? Would she be proud? Relieved to be discovered? Constance frowned, defending herself from other, darker thoughts that she'd rather not entertain. Who knew what today would bring? She was nervous but hopeful.

She slipped out of her bedroom. Downstairs, she could hear the servants in the kitchen, preparing for the day. She tiptoed down the stairs and across the entrance hall, letting herself silently out of the house.

Alexandre was waiting on the other side of the villa, where the rowboat sat under a cover made of coconut-palm leaves. He was pacing, his back turned to her. She said his name softly, and he turned, smiling with relief.

"You came," he said.

"Of course."

"I was worried that something would go wrong."

"Nothing's going to go wrong," she declared. "We are the King and Queen of Today."

He pressed her against him, kissing her behind the ear. "I saw Maitland leave the pearler ten minutes ago. We should hurry."

They dragged the boat to the water's edge. Constance climbed in, and Alexandre pushed it into the water, leaping in and grabbing the oars. They arrowed out through the harbor as the sun hesitated behind the horizon. Constance stifled a vast yawn.

"Tired?"

"I didn't sleep."

"Nor me. Too much to think about. Today is . . ." He didn't say it, but the idea hung between them. Their last day together.

A flock of seagulls circled overhead. The morning breeze was fresh, plucking at her clothes and hair. Mingled excitement and sadness threaded through her, as the beach disappeared behind them. Soon, they were tying the rowboat, climbing aboard *La Reine des Perles*. Alexandre showed her quickly where everything was, then wound in the anchor. He seemed so strong and capable— his feet bare, his trousers rolled to his knees—that she was momentarily distracted from the task at hand. But Alexandre began shouting orders at her as the sun rose, and the ship was readied to sail. Finally, he told Constance to take the wheel, while he managed the ropes that controlled the sails. One by one, they were hauled up, the wind flapping them, the sun staining them orange. He pulled them and tied them, and their bellies filled. Constance could feel the ship straining beneath her hands, as anxious to get away as she was. Slowly, slowly, they began to move. Away from the harbor and towards the hidden temple of Ranumaran.

Chapter 18

Three hours out of Nagakodi, the area began to look familiar to Alexandre, and he was lost in thought as he tried to remember if he had been there before. He held the wheel as the pearler bounced along the choppy waters. The sun dazzled on the sails. Constance was as useful and strong as any crewman, but that was no surprise if her father was a sailor. Even if he'd never taught her a thing, that kind of sea-courage was passed along in the blood.

"You're very quiet," she said, leaning on the railing opposite him.

"I'm trying to remember. I think I've been here before. With de Locke. When I was just a lad."

"Really? So do you think you've seen Ranumaran before too?"

"I'm not sure. De Locke never told me where we were going; we just went." His eyes caught on a rocky outcrop in the distance, almost like the face of an ape. "Yes, I'm certain I've sailed up here before. We've hunted for pearls all through the Gulf."

"Tell me about de Locke," she asked, turning so that her back was against the railing.

Alexandre shook his head. "I don't even know how to start."

"Why did you choose to work with him?"

"There was no choice. He acquired my services in France when I was only a boy. He was good to me, I suppose. Even gentle. As long as I did as he said, we had no conflict. He taught me to read and brought me books and drawing paper. He never paid me, but I ate well enough and always had a safe place to sleep."

"Were you like a son to him? A protégé?"

Alexandre laughed bitterly. "I never made the mistake of thinking he had any fond feelings for me." But her words provoked the memory: de Locke shaking with rage, the pistol at Alexandre's temple. *Alexandre, how could you?* De Locke had been angry about more than the theft of the pearl; he had been angry that Alexandre had betrayed him.

"And for your part? Did you have any fond feelings towards him?"

"I did at the start," Alexandre conceded. "But we do

not stay forever children, Constance. Knowledge comes with age, although it's not always welcome."

"Do you think knowledge really comes with age? Then that would make my father a very knowledgeable man."

"He is."

She tilted her head, irritation crossing her brow. "And yet, he'd rather I married Victor Kloppman than you."

"We are all constrained by our circumstances."

"You are so forgiving of my father."

"He was forgiving of me."

"Not in the end."

"He was forgiving of me as far as he could be. I understand." He paused, watching her a moment. "Constance, if you find your mother, what do you think will happen next?"

Her eyes went to the horizon. "I don't know. I have this fantasy: we rescue her and take her back to Father. He forgives everything, even us. But as to what will really happen . . ." She paused here. "I think it would satisfy me just to look on her face," she said softly. "I have waited so long."

As they rounded a curve in the land, the vertical summit of Sun Peak came into view. "God willing, your wait will soon be over. I believe we are scarce two miles from our goal." For a reason he couldn't articulate, he began to feel tense. Perhaps it was because he suspected Constance would be disappointed. Either they wouldn't find Faith Blackchurch at all, or they would find her and she would not be as Constance hoped. He had heard enough of the people of Nagakodi complain about a sharp-tongued, cruel-tempered woman. Or perhaps the tension was simply because he knew today would be the last hours they spent together.

But neither of those explanations seemed right, so he bent his mind back again to his childhood, to the time when he and de Locke had been here before. He peered into the distance, looking for landmarks. A shimmer of white ahead on the water caught his eye.

And he remembered.

"Get down!" he shouted to Constance. "I'm going to have to gybe." He remembered how he and de Locke had only just missed it, a jagged ridge of rock perfectly visible at low tide, but cruelly lying in wait when the tide was high. And, once more, *La Reine des Perles* was headed directly for it at speed. "There's a reef ahead. It will tear us in two."

Constance flattened herself on the deck, and Alexandre hauled the wheel as hard as he could. There was no time to sheet in. The ship shuddered underneath him; he felt huge resistance. Normally, he was very cool in a crisis, but the instinct to protect Constance was overwhelming. As they turned, the sails crashed around—first the headsail, then the foremast sail, with a huge crack. Splinters flew off the mast. All the booms swung fast and sudden, sweeping savagely across the deck, skidding above Constance's head. His heart thundered. The pearler, grinding against its trajectory, came around. She was out of control now, and the main sheets were a tangle, hooked around the boom crutch.

"Constance," he called, wrestling with the ropes, "can you release the jib sheet?"

She leapt to her feet and loosened the rope, and the pearler began to settle. The shallow breaking waves over the rocks skidded past to starboard. He held his breath against the possibility that some deeper submerged rocks might catch them, then released it again as they sailed into the clear.

Constance collapsed to her knees with relief. "I thought we were done for."

"Of course we're not done for," he said with a wry smile. "We are the King and Queen of Today." He examined the damage to the main mast, feeling a pang of guilt for Captain Blackchurch. It wouldn't take much to repair, and it certainly wouldn't stop them sailing home. A lucky escape.

And now, a little village came into view. A collection of thatch huts huddled between coconut palms. Dotting the shallows were men on fishing stilts, their lines cast into the water. In the distance, three small vessels bobbed in the water at anchor.

Constance looked around. "That's it, isn't it? That's Ranumaran."

"I think so."

She pointed back behind them, towards the coastline. "I saw a cave near the reef. I think it's the hidden temple."

"I will check Nissanka's map, but I think you are right."

"Can we anchor here?" she said. "I've waited sixteen years; I can't wait another moment."

Henry took his breakfast in the library, trying to save time in the day. He had some correspondence to write for Howlett before the buyer arrived to look over the pearler. Birds twittered in the garden, and the sea breeze gently troubled his papers on the desk. He put a paperweight on them and turned to the morning's mail. Usually, it was only business and general correspondence for Howlett, but today he saw immediately the one addressed to him. He slit it open, expecting another letter full of disappointments. He'd had more than a dozen that began, *Dear Sir, I regret that I do not have any information to add.* . . . It seemed he had chased Faith as far as he could, and he was already preparing himself for the trip home.

But this letter expressed no regrets, and Henry found his blood jumped when he read the first few lines.

Dear Sir,

Thank you for your correspondence concerning the disposal of furniture against debts in Nagakodi, September 1789. I appreciate that you have spent some time in the hunt for these details, and it is only through coincidence that I am able to write to you with some information that may help you. As the office of the debt register no doubt told you, many records were lost in the flood of 1793. However, I was, in fact, one of the debtors owed and had dealings with Mrs. Blackchurch, or Faith Wicks as she was known to me.

Henry paused here, his mind spinning. Faith Wicks? She had adopted *that* name? The insult was too great to bear. He took a breath and continued.

I lent her money on her arrival in Nagakodi, directly before I moved to another post at Mannar in 1785. I had a good deal of correspondence with Mrs. Wicks over the repayment of the debt, a debt that she was either unwilling or unable to honor. The last I heard of Mrs. Wicks, she had plans to come to Mannar. She offered to repay me in full, in person, if I would assist her in finding a place to live and a post in service where she might be able to earn a small income for herself. I have enclosed that letter for your information. I have retained all the correspondence, should you desire to possess it, but it is certainly only of a business nature.

Again, Henry had to pause. The idea of Faith in service to anyone . . . it was unimaginable. She had too much pride, surely. Things must have gone very badly for her. He didn't know what to feel. Pity? Anger? He returned to the letter.

Mrs. Wicks told me she would be arriving within one week. She was to take the journey north on a ship called the Monkey King. *That ship never arrived, and I did not hear from her again until her furniture was sold and I was forwarded a small amount of money, less than a fifth of what she owed me.*

I am very sorry that this is all the information I have for you. As there are barely sixty miles of coast between Nagakodi and Mannar, it is not unthinkable that a local might have heard of her, or of the Monkey King. *I cannot say, however, whether you should be satisfied in your search if your goal is to bring your wife home to England with you. You will forgive me for speaking frankly.*

Yours,

Ernest Carver Esq.

Henry turned to the letter from Faith. It detailed only what Carver had said; there was no hidden meaning to squeeze from the words. But he stared at it a long time nonetheless. It was in her handwriting, the only thing he possessed that she had touched after her disappearance from his life.

Faith Wicks. He knew now why she had disappeared.

It was as his sister Violet had suspected and, although she had warned him, the dashing of his hopes was spectacularly painful.

He hadn't long to nurse his feelings though, as the door opened quietly and Chandrika stood there, an anxious expression on her brow.

"Yes?" he said, clearing his throat, folding up the letter neatly.

"Captain Blackchurch, Miss Constance and Miss Orlanda both failed to come down to breakfast. I checked their rooms, and they are both empty."

"Empty?" He pushed back his chair but didn't rise. "Well, they must be somewhere together, concocting some nonsense. What do Mr. and Mrs. Howlett say?"

"They told me to come and ask if you knew anything."

A prickle of unease. Orlanda was wild, but surely she couldn't have compelled Constance to do anything too foolish. "I know nothing."

"Thank you, sir. I shall report back to you if I hear any news."

Henry stood and began to pace. He moved to the French doors and gazed into the garden. Constance was cross with him, that was for certain. But she was a reasonable young woman.

Wasn't she?

The door to the library burst open behind him, this time without an accompanying knock. He turned and saw Maitland standing there, flushed and shoeless.

"Captain, the *Queen of Pearls* is gone!"

"Gone? How can it be gone? You were aboard it." He noticed that sand clung to Maitland's coat and trousers, and groaned. "A bad night for sleeping on the beach, Maitland. I have a buyer coming today, all the way from Colombo. He hoped to sail her back this afternoon."

"I'm sorry, sir."

"The question is, how on earth are those two ninnies sailing it? Constance knows her way around the ropes, but Orlanda doesn't strike me as—"

"Orlanda?" he said. "Orlanda's here. She's been . . ." He lowered his voice. "She's been with me."

"Then how . . . ? Constance couldn't sail the pearler single-handed. . . ." Dawning realization. His heart fell all the way to his feet, and he pressed his hand against his forehead in the hopes it would still his thoughts. "Alexandre, of course," he muttered. He was paralyzed, afraid to move or breathe. It was happening again: the woman he loved, disappearing into the dawn.

Maitland grew uncomfortable with the long silence.

"Sir? What do you want me to do?"

"Ready *Good Bess* for immediate departure. We have about an hour before the tide dips too low."

"But where will we go? We don't even know which direction they've gone in. South, north, across to India?"

Henry's voice grew strident with rage. "Yes, yes, they could be *anywhere* in the world. I am well aware of this, Maitland, as I am well aware that you were *anywhere* when you should have been *somewhere*, and that was aboard that damn pearler. Find Orlanda; she might know something. And send Chandrika to search Constance's room." He slammed his fists on the writing desk, making the inkpot jump. "We have to find my daughter."

<hr/>

The beach at Ranumaran was not as pleasant as the one at Nagakodi. A thin strip, gravelly rather than fine sand. With Nissanka's map in her hand, Constance and Alexandre found their way back towards the reef that had almost claimed *La Reine des Perles*, to find the cave.

Already, she was preparing herself for disappointment. In her imagination, the hidden temple had been a roomy system of underground tunnels. Habitable, of course, even cozy, with the warm ocean roaring just beyond its front door. But the opening of the cave she had seen was small and dark. Alexandre led the way, leading her up on rocks. She was careful not to cut her feet, using her toes to cling to the hard surface. Then they were there.

Dank. Poky. No tunnels leading off to hidden places. Simply a cave that smelled of dead fish and old seaweed, around five feet high at the entrance, just tall enough to stand within, though not for Alexandre, who had to duck. The let-down was acute, almost taking her breath away.

Alexandre picked up a stick of driftwood and moved around the cave, poking at the walls. "I can't see any tunnels," he said.

"That's because there are no tunnels," she sighed. "This is it. The hidden temple of Ranumaran. A stinking little cave in the cliff face." She sank down to sit on a flat rock near the cave entrance. Half a beam of sunlight fell into her lap. "I've brought you all this way, caused all of this trouble, for nothing."

Alexandre sat next to her, and together they watched the sea break over the reef for a few minutes. "I'm sorry that you are disappointed, Constance," he said. "But I am not sorry I came with you."

She turned to him and admired his profile. Then he

turned, smiled at her, and leaned in to kiss her. "Dear Constance," he murmured against her hair.

"What now, Alexandre?" She pulled her knees up and grasped them.

"Remind me again what Nissanka said."

Constance screwed her eyes shut, turning the memory over in her mind. "He said an Englishman came here every day for years; he would stay for an hour and then go again. Though who he was, I've no idea. I had thought he was visiting Mother. That perhaps he had constrained her somehow, or . . . perhaps she knew him. He was taking care of her. I don't know. But Mother wasn't here. Nobody could live here."

"So why did he come?"

"To meet her? Perhaps she came from somewhere else?"

"But why here? Why would anybody come here to meet? There are many other, nicer places. Safer, without rocks everywhere. There must be something about this place particularly."

"Nissanka said the locals thought he was praying. They said it was his temple, because he told them he went there for faith. For Faith."

Alexandre mused, watching the water. Constance

couldn't think straight, reality rushing in on her. She would have to go back, explain herself to her father, and say goodbye to Alexandre forever. *All for nothing.*

"Constance?" he said, at length, in a very gentle voice that made her frightened, because why would he speak so gently unless he feared hurting her?

"Yes?"

"Look out from the cave. What do you see?"

She turned her eyes out. "The sea."

"You can see the sea from anywhere along the coast. What can you see from right here?"

She looked again. "The reef."

He turned his sad gaze to her, and realization began to dawn on her. Tears pricked her eyes.

"I'm so sorry, Constance," he said. "But I think I know what happened to your mother."

"No, Alexandre," she said, because she didn't know what else to say.

"That reef is barely visible until you're on top of it. It would be so easy for a ship to sail right into it. In bad weather, or at night, getting out of the water and onto land would be near impossible. Perhaps possible for a man, a strong swimmer. But for an English woman with little experience of the sea . . ." He took her hand in his. "The strong swimmer would never forgive himself, especially if he loved her. He would return, again and again, to the place he lost her. To pray, in a way. To be near her."

Tears began to fall. "But there must be a chance—she couldn't have been dead all this time."

"I'm sorry, Constance." He put his arms around her and she clung to him, sobbing. Years of dreams dissolved around her, leaving her with the harsh, brutal possibility.

She sat back, palming tears from her eyes. "But we don't know for certain, do we?" she said again. "We're only guessing."

"I can find out for certain if you like," he said. "I can swim out there and dive for the wreckage."

Her heart was at once torn: it sounded like a dangerous endeavour, but she wanted badly to know for certain. If her mother was dead, then so be it. She could tell Father, and they could abandon their search. But if there was even the shred of a possibility . . .

"Is it risky?" she asked quietly.

"Not for me. I'm a strong swimmer; I can hold my breath for nearly six minutes." He stroked her fingers. "I should like to do you one last favor, to repay you for everything you've done for me."

"Everything I've done?"

"You've brought me a joy I hadn't thought possible in my life. And that is worth repaying."

She squeezed his hand. "As long as you promise to be very safe and come back to my arms whole and unharmed."

"I promise."

"Go on then. See what you can find."

De Locke unfolded his weary body from the ground where he had slept the previous night. The sun was already well overhead and had pierced through a gap in the leaves, and he realized the left side of his face was sunburnt. One more irritation to add to the long list. He had only managed to escape the skipper of the fish boat through speed, not guile. De Locke had run off while he was unloading his baskets, plunged into the jungle, and kept running until he was sure the skipper had given up on his payment. A jungle at night wasn't the best place to sleep, so he'd made his way towards the sound of the ocean and found some grass near the edge of the beach. He had tossed and turned for hours before finally catching sleep on the verge of dawn.

Then slept long enough to get sunburnt.

He scratched at the row of mosquito bites all up his arm. There was an elephant track around here somewhere, but he'd have to head away from the beach to find it. No matter. There were still many hours of daylight left, and he expected to arrive in Nagakodi before sunset. He hoped to find somewhere to drink along the way, and perhaps some tropical fruit or other to ease his hunger pains.

But first, he needed to go down to the sea, to splash salt water on the mosquito bites, which had started to ooze blood. He broke from the cover of the foliage, then stopped in his tracks.

La Reine des Perles.

He rubbed his eyes; it must surely be a hallucination, a trick of his overtired brain. But no, there she was, catching the sunlight on the azure water.

De Locke began to laugh. There was no boat in sight to steal, but she was swimming distance away. He waded out into the sunlit water and began to make his way to his ship.

Chapter 19

Chandrika caught Henry as he emerged from the library, pulling on his coat and readying himself to sail.

"Captain Blackchurch?" she said, urging him back into the library.

"What now, woman?"

She closed the library door behind them, found a note in her apron pocket and gave it to him. "This was under Constance's pillow."

He watched his own hands shake as he unfolded it, as though he were outside himself. He was almost too frightened to read it.

Dear Father,

You are no doubt wondering where I am and what my intentions are. I wish to reassure you that I haven't disappeared as my mother did; I have merely gone on a short adventure, from which I will return—depending on favorable conditions—

before nightfall. I am with Alexandre, who has been of great service to me in my hunt, and whom I trust to keep me safe.

I did not undertake this adventure lightly. You see, I have been conducting my own investigation into Mother's disappearance and have followed my clues to the hidden temple of Ranumaran. There, I hope to discover my mother, and perhaps bring her back with me. I know that if I can do that, I can win back your good favor.

Your loving daughter, Constance.

"Captain Blackchurch?" Chandrika said, anxiously. "Is everything well?"

"She's gone to . . . " His voice caught, and he cleared his throat. "She says she's gone to find her mother." Despair washed over him. "The girl simply wants her mother."

Chandrika wouldn't meet his eye. "She is safe, then?"

"I hope so." He wiped away a traitorous tear, forcing his voice to be bright. "Ranumaran. Not far."

"No sir. But twenty miles."

"We'll sail immediately."

Constance and Alexandre picked their way over the rocky beach to the southern side of the reef. The beach was more sheltered, the water clearer. Alexandre stripped to his trousers and waded into the sea.

"Be careful," Constance called.

"I will." Cautiously, he dunked under the water. The sandy bottom dipped away steeply. Rocks dotted it. He launched himself forward and began to swim, stopping every few feet to check the position of rocks. The shadow of the reef and the gully that ran behind it waited in the distance.

Despite what he had told Constance, this was not without its dangers. He didn't know the waters, the rocks were cruel, and there was always the danger of sharks. But neither was it inherently risky, especially for Alexandre, who had proved almost impossible to drown. He made his way through the warm water, a safe distance from the reef, then over into the gully.

The depth increased steeply again, the bottom a murky swirl below him. He shot to the surface, took a slow deep breath, waved once to Constance, then dived.

Down and down. Not on a stone and a rope this time, but simply with the weight of his own body. Sunlight shafted the water, but it was much cooler down here.

He saw the front half of a ship almost straightaway.

It was bow up, pointing accusingly at the reef that had caused the damage. Alexandre could see a gulf opening up behind it, a final steep drop-off. He swam to the bow, brushing off algae and seaweed. Fish darted in and out of a large hole, but he could see enough letters to know this was Faith Blackchurch's ship.

. . . NKEY KI . . .

The *Monkey King*. He made his way up to the surface, the last of his breath squeezing tightly. Took another breath without facing the beach where Constance waited. He should just go now, swim back to her, tell her he had seen the shipwreck. She would be devastated; if only he could bring back for her something from the wreck, something to ease her sorrow. And so he dived again.

He swam down to the wreck and examined the *Monkey King*'s swollen ribs. It was a jumbled mess of wreckage, splintered wood, brass black with algae, eels snaking around, barnacles attached to everything. He made out a wooden chair with only two legs, and swam towards it, picking in the debris around it. A dinner plate, a hairbrush. He kept sorting the junk, his lungs protesting that he was taking too long.

Then he saw it. A delicate thread, too easy to mistake for a piece of seaweed. But it didn't dance on the water; it hung. It was heavy. It was made of gold.

Alexandre pulled the necklace free. On the end of it was a round locket. He wrapped the chain around his wrist, swam hard towards the surface, and broke the water gasping for air.

Then, when his lungs felt balanced again, he slowly made his way back to Constance.

———

Constance paced anxiously, letting out half her breath when she saw Alexandre surface safely and the other half when he climbed out of the water. He pushed his wet hair off his face and said in a breathy voice, "I'm sorry, Constance. I found the *Monkey King* down there."

"Mother's ship," she said.

"Yes."

The tide of despair made her collapse forward. Alexandre caught her and held her while she sobbed. She was aware that he was making her dress damp, but cared nothing for it. Mother was dead. There would be no reunion, no words of kindness and wisdom. She let the desolation roll over her as she cried into Alexandre's warm shoulder.

He gently pushed her away. "Constance, do you recognize this?"

She looked down. Wrapped around his wrist was a chain with a locket. It was green, filthy, but she would have known it anywhere. The locket her mother wore in the portrait at home. Shaking, she unwound it from his arm, scraping the algae off with her thumbnail. She held up the locket to the sun, remembering her long-held fantasy, that there was a picture of herself within. Curious fingers fiddled with the latch. It popped open.

No picture of a baby. Instead, a miniature oil of a man she didn't know. For a few moments, her brain tried to reorganize the man's features into Father's; but he was fair and blue-eyed, with a narrow nose. Nothing like Father. Then who was he?

"Constance?"

The question popped onto her lips unbidden. "Do you think my mother loved me, Alexandre?" she asked.

She was prepared for him to answer as anyone else might have: all mothers love their children. But he didn't. He said, "I do not know. My mother was very unkind; perhaps yours was too."

She showed him the portrait. "I don't know who this man is. I was rather hoping to find a picture of myself."

Part of her wanted to take the portrait of the stranger as confirmation that this was not her mother's locket. But she knew that she would be lying to herself. Her mother had willingly disappeared, had willingly left Constance behind, for this stranger. Her world shifted on its axis, and she turned away from the light of the sun. The fact of her mother's death was one thing to mourn, but the proof that her mother didn't love her . . . She was numb.

"I will have to tell Father," she said. "I don't know how he'll take such news. But I shouldn't wait any longer to break it to him."

"Come, we'll make our way back." He took her hand. The small gesture brought fresh tears. He was the only warm and solid thing left in her world, and at the other end of this journey, she had to let him go. She would drift without him, at the mercy of wind and weather.

"Time for tears later, Constance," he said, pulling gently on her hand. "You need to speak with your father."

Alexandre helped Constance out of the boat and back up the rope to the pearler's deck. She had only a moment to register the warmth of his hands before a shadow fell over them both. She gasped. A large, red-haired man had a pistol cocked and pointed at Alexandre's head.

"Hello, Gilbert," Alexandre said.

"Who's the girl?" the man asked in French.

"She is a friend," Alexandre responded.

Constance, whose French was poor but good enough to understand this conversation, piped up in English. "I am Constance Blackchurch. My father is a well-respected merchant seaman and will be most offended and horrified at your treatment of Alexandre. Point that pistol away from him immediately."

De Locke grinned, turning the pistol on her. "Certainly, Miss Blackchurch," he said with a heavy accent.

Her heart stopped, her panicky bluster evaporating as pure, cold fear iced her veins.

"You have just given me the most splendid idea," de Locke continued. "Alexandre, I can't sail this vessel single-handedly. You will do whatever I say, or I will shoot your companion. Do you understand?"

Alexandre nodded wordlessly. He was ashen with fear. Constance had not imagined he could be so afraid, and his fear intensified her own.

"Set the sails for heading south, back to Nagakodi. I have new business with Henry Blackchurch."

"What do you intend?" Constance cried.

"You will find out in good time. Meanwhile, put your hands together so that I can tie them up." He smiled cruelly. "You may wish to pray."

———

It took forever to get his crew moving. Five of them were ashore, and Henry had little hope of finding them quickly. The others, dismayed by the lack of warning, seemed to have forgotten everything they knew and fumbled their way through tasks so slowly that Henry began to believe he would miss the tide and have to sit here in the harbor and wait for Constance to return on her own.

Finally, finally, they were away, doing their best to catch the reluctant winds. Maitland, who until now had been overflowing with apologies, took the wheel without another word and seemed determined to win back his captain's favor with good work.

Henry walked up and down the poop as they sailed into the heat of the morning, worried not so much about Constance but about what she might find. Was it possible that Faith had settled in Ranumaran? Was she living a simple life, the life of a fisherman's wife? How would such a life etch itself on her beautiful face and hands? He knew now that she would not want to return with him. In truth, she had never really wanted to be with him. Even on their wedding day, she had cried. Not with joy, he knew that. She had been only eighteen, barely older than Constance. The marriage was considered appropriate for her. Her parents had been keen on the match; Henry had been utterly smitten. Faith's own reluctance had never figured in the equation. He had convinced himself she would grow to love him. Within two years, when her eyes seemed to turn constantly elsewhere, he had realized his mistake. But he hadn't been able to stop loving her. Even when she disappeared—when Violet, his close friends, even her family had suggested that she might have left willingly—he hadn't been able to think so ill of her. He had reserved a little piece of himself to trust her, to hope for her return. They'd had Constance, after all. Divinely precious proof of love.

"Sir?" It was the second officer, Hickey, rousing him from his reverie.

"Yes?"

"We've spied a vessel off our starboard bow. It's the *Queen of Pearls*."

He folded his arms, embarrassed to have his crew see him out chasing his errant daughter. "Good. When she's a good distance to parley, I'll go across and have a word with her new skipper."

"Do you want us to ready the cannons?"

"That won't be necessary," he said, the hot flush of embarrassment creeping up his neck. "My daughter's on board."

"Your . . . ?"

"Not another word," he said sternly.

Hickey nodded and headed off, calling commands to slow down, ready to pull up alongside the schooner.

———

Constance's hands were tied tightly in front of her. She had been compelled to sit on the deck, while Alexandre had to manage the sheets, which he did quietly and coolly. She wished she could read his thoughts. Her own were in turmoil. She knew only a little about de Locke and didn't know if he was dangerous or merely a fool. She veered from terrified thoughts of Alexandre's death, or her own, to semi-calm acceptance that he would put them ashore soon, then sail off in the vessel he thought belonged to him. Nonetheless, she felt useless just waiting, so she began to work away at the stitches in the hem of her skirt. If she could free the pearl, perhaps she could convince de Locke to leave them be. He was angry at Alexandre; perhaps this was the reason. Perhaps once he had it, he would be satisfied. Her fingernails picked at the cotton, slowly and carefully, stitch by stitch.

But before she had the chance to work it completely free, de Locke called to Alexandre in French, "I see the English pig's ship."

Constance turned and searched the sea with her eyes. There she was, *Good Bess*, sails set steadfastly, powering through the waves towards them. She sighed inwardly with relief. Never had she been so glad to see her father.

"Hove to," de Locke said to Alexandre. "I will speak with him."

The pearler slowed, then stopped moving forward. She waited on the motion of the waves, as *Good Bess* loomed closer.

"It would be best if they don't see me," de Locke said to Alexandre, indicating with a tilt of his head the hatch that led below deck. "But you can be sure, I will come up to talk to Blackchurch when I am ready, and any attempts by you to escape will mean certain death for his daughter. Do you understand?"

Alexandre nodded mutely. De Locke pulled Constance to her feet and arranged her so she stood beside Alexandre, hanging his coat over her hands so that her bonds could not be seen. "Come now, child. Smile for Papa." Then he turned and went down the first three steps to the cabin, waiting in the dark.

Good Bess was close enough now that Constance could see her father on the poop deck high above them. She couldn't make out his expression, but suspected he was frowning. She tried to smile, but couldn't. She wanted to sob, but didn't.

His voice came over the speaking trumpet. "Constance, I am coming over in a boat. You are to climb into it immediately. Maitland will assist Alexandre in sailing the ship back to Nagakodi."

She nodded that she had heard. De Locke snickered in his hole. Now Constance grew terrified. Of what was this man capable? Would he hurt Father? She realized, suddenly and clearly, that she wouldn't feel safe in the world if she lost Father.

Over on *Good Bess*, the boat was lowered into the water, with Father, Maitland and Hickey inside. They began to row across the narrow space between the ships. De Locke waited until they were only twenty feet away, then uncoiled from his hiding place, brandishing his pistol. "Good afternoon, Captain Blackchurch," he shouted over the wind.

Father scrambled to his feet, nearly capsizing the boat.

Maitland pulled him back to his seat. "De Locke! What are you doing with my daughter?"

She didn't see it, but she knew that the pistol was once again pointed at her head, because Father's face was panicked.

"I am interested to know how much her life is worth to you."

Father held up both his hands. "Stop. Do not hurt her. She is worth everything to me. You may keep the *Queen of Pearls*; just let me have my daughter."

De Locke began to laugh so wildly that Constance feared he would fire the pistol by accident. "The pearler? But you said she is worth everything. Much more than this wretched vessel."

Moments passed with no words spoken. Constance could see Father's face working, as realization was upon him.

"Yes, that's right, Blackchurch. You hand over *Good Bess* or Miss Blackchurch is no more."

Constance wanted to call out to him not to listen to de Locke, that she had brought this on herself with her impulsiveness, that he must keep his livelihood. But she was afraid, so afraid. She wanted to cling to life at any cost.

De Locke was beckoning Father's boat grandly. "Come, come, do not delay. You may take possession of this fine vessel, and I shall take your little boat back to my new ship."

"Are these your only terms, de Locke?" Father asked.

"My only terms."

"Then so be it." He gave the order to continue rowing. Constance's stomach hollowed out with despair.

De Locke laughed, giving Alexandre a companionable punch on the shoulder. "Well done, lad," he said in French. "You've brought me another great success. I was going to kill you, but now I think I'll take you over to *Good Bess* with me."

"I'd rather rot in hell."

De Locke waved the pistol. "Be careful, lad. I can grant such a wish, if you please."

Constance closed her eyes. The world was falling apart around her, and there was nothing she could do. Then she felt a slip, a tickle at her bare ankles as the seam on her hem gave way. The pearl dropped to the deck, and began to roll towards the water.

De Locke's eyes were on it immediately. "What's that? A pearl?" Instinct governing him, he leapt on it, trying to catch it before it plunged into the sea. He was bent over in front of her, his head below the railing. If she kicked him hard enough, there wasn't anything to stop him going straight into the water.

But did she have the courage?

There wasn't time to debate it. She stepped forward and planted her foot in his behind. He sprawled forward, discharging his gun in the air, reaching around with his free hand to grab her ankle. The ship heeled, they both fell.

Into the water.

Bubbles fizzed around her. Her hands were tied; she had no way of making her way towards the surface. She struggled, frantic. De Locke was nearby, kicking towards sunlight, but she was spinning further and further away from light and air.

"Constance!" Henry clambered to the side of the boat, leaning over so far he nearly overbalanced.

"Sir, be careful," Maitland said.

Henry pulled off his jacket, readying himself to jump in the water, when he heard a splash near the pearler. Alexandre had gone in. Could he trust the lad? Probably. But de Locke was still under there somewhere, so he dived in as well, while his two officers sat as though their behinds were glued in the boat.

Darkness descended on Constance. She breathed the sea. She felt her lungs would burst.

Strong arms caught her. She was being pulled upwards. *Too late*, she thought. *I'm already dead.* But then sunlight broke over her, and she was coughing and coughing as water, made hot by her body, poured from her nose and mouth.

"It's all right, I have you," Alexandre said, pressing her against him. "I have you."

Henry began to swim towards the place he had seen Constance disappear. Alexandre still hadn't surfaced. Then, the water broke and de Locke launched himself upwards, growling like a tiger. It caught Henry unawares, and he spluttered in the water as de Locke grabbed him in a headlock and pushed him under. De Locke used his free hand to punch Henry's nose. Blood spurted; stars flew before his eyes. Henry got his hands around de Locke's arm and clawed at his skin to no avail. He struggled, managing to get his nose above water long enough to see Alexandre drag Constance up and swim her towards the row boat. Arms reached out to help her in. A sensible boy, Henry thought, strangely detached from his circumstances. Now that Constance was safe, it didn't seem to matter so much that de Locke was wrestling his face into the water, that the world was going to continue without him. He relaxed, prepared for whatever would come.

What came was an almighty *thwack*. De Locke fell away, limp, and disappeared under the water. Alexandre, aboard the row boat, stood braced against the seat, holding out an oar.

"Captain," he said. "Take hold."

Henry, exhausted, hooked his elbow over the oar and allowed himself to be pulled to safety.

Chapter 20

Constance sat, still damp, on the bed in her cabin aboard *Good Bess*, waiting for Father to return. She was weary, tired of worrying. What he did with Alexandre, the pearler, his officers . . . it hardly mattered. The adventure was over, and for once she wanted circumstances to wash over her, instead of trying so hard to control them.

A knock at her cabin door, then Father was there. He had changed into dry clothes, but his hair was still wet, combed back from his forehead.

"I looked," he said, "but could find no dry clothes for you."

"I'll survive," she said.

He sat at the table, arms folded. Was wordless for long moments. Finally, he said, "I do not know where to start, Constance."

"I do." She took a deep breath and unclasped the locket from around her neck to hand to him. "I am sorry, Father, but I know now that Mother is dead. Her ship, the

Monkey King, was wrecked off Ranumaran. Alexandre dived the wreck. He found this."

His movements slowed as he took it; his brow softened. "Ah," he said. "I see."

She let him sit silently. The ship pitched gently.

"I'm sorry," she said again.

"I'm sorry, too, child. I . . . don't know what to think. She has been absent for sixteen years, but final confirmation of her death . . . "

"I know precisely how you feel," she blurted, glad to have somebody understand her. "There was always hope, but now there is just . . . "

"Acceptance."

"Yes," she said softly. Then, "Father, who is the man in the portrait?"

"Which portrait?"

She approached him and flicked open the locket. "This one."

Father's eyebrows twitched. He closed the locket and offered it back to her, but she shook her head. He placed it, instead, in his pocket. "His name was Donald Wicks. A business associate of mine. I knew he had feelings for Faith, so I ended all contact with him a year before her disappearance. I expected that would be an end to it."

"So she ran off with him?"

"It would appear so."

"And she left us behind? You. And me."

Father stood and took her wrists in his hands. "Her actions were not your fault, Constance," he said, reading her thoughts.

"But if she only loved me . . . " she began, tears overflowing again. "I must have been a hateful child. Illtempered. Sleepless."

"No, no. Constance, you were a bonny baby. You charmed whomever you saw. Oh, I loved to squeeze your little fat arms. You were so precious to me. . . . You still are, my dear."

Constance reined in her tears.

"As to whether she loved you, I don't know, Constance. Perhaps she loved the idea of her freedom more. But you *were* loved. By Violet. By me." He released her arms and walked away, pausing by the dresser, lost in thought.

She sensed a softening in him and decided to take advantage of it. "Father, what are you going to do with Alexandre?"

He turned, his brows drawn down. "Do not turn your mind to this nonsense. . . . "

"Only he has lost his pearl," she continued as though

she hadn't heard. "He has no way of getting home now."

"Alexandre is in the cattle pen, waiting for me to decide what to do with him. Theft of a ship is a serious offense."

"He didn't steal a ship," she bit back, irritated with his suddenly pompous tone. "He helped me sail it. You know that. You know he's a good man. How can you bear to be so constrained by propriety? It is not reasonable!"

Father didn't answer, and a long silence drew out, broken only by the sound of the waves splashing on the hull of the ship.

"Father?"

"You must get him out of your head, Constance," he said softly.

"I can't. I love him."

"I know you *think* you love him, but you are young and—"

"I *do* love him. He is noble and clever and brave. Do you deny that too? For he saved *your* life, while Maitland and Hickey sat there like slugs on a rock."

Father straightened his back. "I shan't endure this conversation another moment. We will be anchoring in less than an hour. Ready yourself." He left, closing the door behind him.

Alexandre sat in the straw, going over his situation in his mind. His pearl, hunted for years, had disappeared into the sea along with de Locke. Now they rested together at the bottom of the ocean. Not only must he endure Constance's departure, but he also had little chance of returning home.

And yet, he could regret nothing. Those last few moments on the beach at Ranumaran, holding her while she cried, the aching tenderness, were imprinted on his memory.

A footstep nearby caught his attention. He looked up to see Captain Blackchurch approaching him in the gloom. Alexandre stood, nodded in deference.

"I owe you a very great deal, Alexandre," he said.

"I did what any man would do," he replied.

Captain Blackchurch smiled ruefully. "My own men didn't do it."

"They would have, sir, had I not jumped in first."

The captain rubbed his palms together and seemed to be considering something. "I will find you a way home, Alexandre, if that is what you want."

"It is, sir."

"Are you certain? Life will be very different in Europe.

Shoes. Manners. Not running off with your employer's daughter."

Alexandre dropped his gaze. "I love Ceylon. I love the raw beauty. But I do not belong here. One should endeavour, as much as possible, to stay out of places one doesn't belong."

"Come now. Where would England be if she stayed out of places she didn't belong?" the captain said with a smile. "Well, Alexandre, I will see what I can arrange for you. I have friends in Colombo; somebody will find you a ship to work your passage home."

"I don't know how to thank you, Captain."

"It's easy," he replied. "You stay away from my daughter."

Orlanda was waiting on the beach when Constance was rowed up to shore.

"I was so worried about you!" she twittered, enclosing Constance in a tight squeeze.

Constance was taken aback. It had been only a day since their terrible argument.

Orlanda locked Constance's hand in her own and pulled her up the beach, still chattering. "Only, when you disappeared with Alexandre I realized how beastly I'd been, and I confessed *all* to Father. Everything. He was so disappointed in me, so very stern! But he admitted that he has been rather too busy to watch me, and I suggested he needed to employ a man to help with correspondence and so on . . . you'll never guess whom he's asked."

Constance, finally freed from the barrage of words, shook her head, puzzled. "No. Who?"

Orlanda stopped, turning to her with a smile. Dusk gathered around them, bringing a cool breeze off the sea. "Francis Maitland!" Orlanda said. "On my recommendation of course." Orlanda turned her eyes to *Good Bess*. "He's been growing weary of following your father around for some time now, but don't tell your father yet. I think Francis wants to wait until he's in a good mood."

"He might be waiting a long time," Constance muttered.

"In any case, I am sorry, Constance," she said, resuming their walk up the beach towards the villa.

"And I am sorry too. I am especially sorry for misleading you and officer Maitland with the notes."

Orlanda tapped her hand playfully. "There is nothing to apologize for. I should thank you. Tonight, after supper, I shall tell you all about Francis and me."

Constance stretched her back, yawning. The events of

the day had caught up with her. She wanted to take a warm bath, climb into her nightgown, and curl up to sleep. "I am so very tired, Orlanda. Perhaps tomorrow?"

Orlanda bit her tongue. "Of course. Tomorrow will be fine."

Henry couldn't sleep. He was weary to his bones, but sleep wouldn't come. Finally, he rose from his bed and went to the window. He could hear the sea, and he listened for a while, letting its rhythms soothe him. The beauty of the sea, his truest passion. The horizon forever running away from him, always and always. How he loved to chase that horizon.

It was little surprise that he was still awake. His mind turned over and over on itself, the way a piece of seaweed tumbles in a wave. Constance and Faith. The way he had felt that morning when he believed Constance had run away. The way he had felt that afternoon when he accepted that Faith was dead, that he would never be able to ask her the hundred questions he needed answers to.

Something troubled him, and he couldn't put his finger precisely on what it was. It had to do with Constance, with the future. Was he being a blind old fool? Had he lost sight of what was important?

Leaning on the window sill, he turned his face to the stars and made up his mind.

———

At sunset the next day, Constance was up in her room, folding her dresses to place them in her little bag. The pearler had been sold that morning; Father's business here was finished. Soon he would ask her to gather her things and get aboard *Good Bess*. The next favorable tide would take them out of the harbor and towards home. She had little to gather, but it made her feel useful to do something. It kept her mind from being drawn into sad thoughts.

She was surprised by a knock at the door.

"Come in," she called.

Father opened the door. "In the library, please, immediately." Then he backed away.

She put down the dress she was folding and, puzzled, followed him. In the library, she found Alexandre. He was sitting on the sofa, looking as confused as she was. Guilt made her fearful. Had Father heard reports of the kisses she and Alexandre had shared? Were there to be more punishments?

Father closed the door and turned to them with a serious expression.

"I have heard today that my first officer, Francis Maitland, is to leave my service."

Constance and Alexandre exchanged glances.

Father began to pace. "You two have presented me with quite a challenge," he said. "I am two men. A sentimental one and a sensible one. I know, all too well, how a match made to suit the needs of society can have disastrous consequences. And yet . . . I cannot be the man who allows his daughter to marry a pearl diver."

Constance's heart caught on a hook. Why was Father discussing such things?

"Constance," he said, fixing her in his gaze. "You think I do not hear you or understand you. But I do. You say you love this young man, and he is certainly worthy of your love. Alexandre, I presume you return these feelings?"

Alexandre nodded, shocked into silence.

Father stroked his beard. "And yet you are both young."

Alexandre found his voice. "I am nearly twenty, sir."

"Pish. You are *so young*. I have a good second officer, who will make an adequate first officer in Maitland's absence. But I need someone to take Hickey's place. Alexandre, are you interested?"

Alexandre's eyes rounded. "You want me to become your second officer?"

"I do. I want you to sail with me for one year. At the end of that time, if you two still feel the same way about each other, I will allow you to marry."

Constance felt as though she might faint.

Father moved towards the door. "I will give you a moment alone to make your decision." He closed the door behind him.

Constance turned to Alexandre. He smiled and pulled her into his arms. "Is he playing a trick on us?"

"I am certain he isn't."

"What shall we say?"

"I expect we shall say yes."

"It is decided then." He stroked her hair. "I love you so dearly, Constance. How are we to survive, being apart for a year?"

Her heart already lurched at the idea of their separation. "I will keep busy and try not to worry, because you will be in the care of a good man."

Father opened the door unexpectedly, and they jumped apart. He pretended not to see. "Well?" he asked.

"I accept the terms of your offer, Captain Blackchurch," Alexandre said.

"Good," Father said, rocking on the balls of his feet. "Good. We will leave tomorrow morning. Why don't you both go out and enjoy your last Sinhalese sunset? I have some correspondence to deal with."

They escaped into the amber half-light, hand in hand, laughing with joy and relief. It was a few moments before they realized.

"Alexandre, look," Constance said. "No clouds."

"No clouds," he repeated, squeezing her hand in his own.

They stood side by side on the beach and watched the brilliant sun disappear behind the restless sea.

Acknowledgments

Thanks are due to Kate Morton, Nicole Ruckels, Mary-Rose MacColl, Mirko Ruckels, Danielle Rankin, and Elaine Wilkins. Also to the 2007 Year of the Novel cohort, especially Ian Golledge, Nina McGrath, and Rowan Hunt for their wonderful descriptions of nausea. Very special thanks to Ian Wilkins for help with maritime history and other details. All misuses of his carefully researched information I own solely.

K.W.